The Exchange Trip

To Cheryl & Derrick,
for all the grandchildren

ALISON J WAINWRIGHT

x

Copyright © Alison J Wainwright, 2020

All rights reserved.

« **dipitus** »

Dipitus Publishing, Bingley, UK

Set in 11.5/14 pt Garamond

ISBN: 978-1-8380693-0-8

If you would like cost-price copies of
Dipitus titles to sell on behalf of a charity
you're involved with, please visit:
dipitus.wordpress.com/contact

CONTENTS

ACKNOWLEDGEMENTS

Thanks first and foremost to the ancient Latin writer, Lucius Apuleius for his story, *The Transformations of Lucius Apuleius of Madaura*, upon which this book is based.

Thanks to Fiona Meiklejohn, Kenneth Roe, Lisa Rushforth, Leona Deakin, Helder Goncalves and Maggie McGeary for their editorial assistance on this book spanning 19 years!

1 LIVING IN THE PAST

The bus swung round the mountain pass, jerking the pupils on board left and right. Luke Silvester was the latest pupil to vomit into a carrier bag. Miss Trebor and Mrs Mackay were also feeling ill. Not because of the winding road, but because of the acrid stench of the pupils' sick, some of which had arrived before sick bags could be handed out. Mrs Mackay was deeply regretting her involvement in this trip to the Italian Apennines.

Luke and his classmates were also wondering whether the trip was worth it. At first they had been excited about going abroad even though many of them were anxious about having to speak Italian. But after two days on the bus their excitement had worn off. When their travelling amusements had no longer entertained them they had swapped seats and talked to all of their friends until there was nothing more to say. Then they had sung songs about the teachers ('Oh, you'll never get to heaven on Mrs Mackay's knee 'cause Mrs Mackay's knee is all warty') but Mrs Mackay had shut them up with warnings that they were distracting the driver and the bus might crash. That had prompted everyone to fall into a silent nervousness, their heads pressed against the windows in an attempt to catch the tops of the mountains or to gaze, shuddering, into the depths of Northern Italy's ravines. Luke stared out at what lay beyond the ghost-thin reflection in the window of his blue eyes, button nose, golden-brown hair with his cringey ears sticking out, made up for a bit by his tanned skin.

The bus wound round and up and down, and nausea remained rife.

'Nearly there,' Miss Trebor said, as much to reassure the increasingly irate Mrs Mackay as the pupils. Mrs Mackay was becoming convinced that she was being punished for something, sentenced to this never-ending journey from hell. She was getting too old for school trips. Far from being a holiday, they were more challenging than a typical day back at Micklemarsh High School. It was all right for Miss Trebor. She was a newly qualified teacher and as this was her first trip her enthusiasm was not, as yet, sapped. 'Give it a few more days,' she thought.

As the scenery flattened out into a verdant, fertile plain Miss Trebor tried to keep the pupils entertained by telling them again about the region they were staying in, hoping that now they could actually see it, they might pay attention.

'Okay, everyone, listen up. If you look out of the windows, you'll see that we've reached the many vineyards around here.'

'Finally!' breathed Chris Schofield, one of Luke's friends.

Miss Trebor took no notice and went on: 'This area is famous for its wine production and if you remember from your itinerary, we'll be visiting vineyards around Caravalla and finding out how they make the wine. Most of the families you're staying with will own vineyards, although my old friend in Caravalla tells me they've not been doing too well lately. Some Caravallans run general farms as well...' Miss Trebor could see the pupils' attention waning rapidly. 'It's such an exciting opportunity for you all to experience such a radically different and much simpler way of life to yours. And of course, we'll get to see the "Leaning Tower of Pisa" - that'll be exciting... and all the famous art in Florence.'

The class wasn't much impressed by the thought of a load of dark old paintings either. They were wondering why they had to be twinned with a small town in the middle of nowhere instead of a big city or somewhere with a beach. Caravalla was hardly an adventure. And who cared about wine when they couldn't even drink it?

Miss Trebor had visited the Apennines in one of her summer breaks while studying Italian at university. She remembered an interesting story she had heard back then and decided to share it with the pupils.

'As you should know, if you've paid any attention in class, I came here when I was a student and stayed with a local family, just as you're doing. One night, Grandfather Zollo told me a story. I don't remember if the events happened in his lifetime or if the story had been passed down the generations...

'Anyway, it was about a woman called Arianna who ran one of the hotels in Florence. Apparently, she was very competitive and greedy and wanted all of the tourists to choose to stay at her hotel so that she could get rich. She started making up slanderous stories about her competitors. She told the authorities her rivals' kitchens had rats, or that they stole from their guests in the hope their hotels would get closed down or they'd get arrested. Arianna was never successful though because there was never any evidence to support her accusations. She thought of planting some evidence but her neighbours were suspicious of her now and were on their guard so she knew she was bound to get caught.

'The only way Arianna could think of to get rid of her rivals was witchcraft. She went deep into the hills to visit a gypsy camp one day and bought a book about the black arts from them. It wasn't long before she was casting spells on her competitors. She used a binding spell on the entrance to one hotel, which stopped any guests from being able to open the door to go inside. She caused a real infestation of rats at another which got it closed down. For Carlotta and Anna, her most hated rivals, Arianna reserved the best of her magic and turned them into a frog and a goat. That nearly caused her downfall though.

'The townspeople had been suspicious enough of Arianna and when Carlotta and Anna were turned into animals they knew for certain that magic was at work. Anna's husband led a mob to Arianna's door, intending to kill her. The mayor came and managed to talk them into giving Arianna a fair hearing at a trial instead.

'But when the day of the trial came people found that they couldn't leave their houses. Only Arianna could go out; she had cast a spell to bind everyone else to their houses. After a couple of days everyone was quite frightened. They weren't earning any money because they couldn't go to their jobs and they were running out of food. So they bargained for their release by promising Arianna anything she wanted. Arianna revoked the spell and was exempted from her trial and allowed to have the only hotel in the area. And so she grew as rich as she had always dreamed.

'There's no evidence to back the story up, but I suppose there's no evidence to disprove it either. Archaeologists have found ancient scrolls and artefacts which show that people practised witchcraft, though that's not to say that magic exists or, even, that the ancient Romans believed it did. It might just have been a way for people to get their grievances off their chest. Most of us would ridicule the idea of magic today but you'd be surprised how passionately people round here still believe in it.'

Miss Trebor's story seemed to do the trick and the revitalised class spent the last ten minutes of the journey eagerly chatting about the latest horror films and supernatural TV series. The majority of the girls argued in favour of the existence of supernatural powers but the boys, if any of them did believe in magic, were too macho to admit it.

'It's just scary stories made up to frighten people into obeying rules,' Luke's friend Jamie Healey declared. Luke nodded his head in total agreement, still feeling too ill to engage in anything more rigorous.

The pupils were so excitable when they finally did arrive in the town square that Miss Trebor and Mrs Mackay struggled to quieten them down in order to unite them with their hosts. Luke was briefly introduced to his hosts, Riccardo Valli and his daughter, Marcella, before they were all whisked off for an ice-breaking game of football. The Micklemarshers, once they had shaken off their numbness and nausea, beat the Caravallans due to their excess energy from being cooped up on the bus. Then came the dreaded moment when the Micklemarshers went their separate ways with people they didn't know.

Luke was less anxious than his classmates as he was top of the class in Italian. He didn't mind the teasing he got for it because he wasn't very good at much else. Plus, he felt it was cheating really because his granddad was from Italy. Not long after he had learnt to talk as a baby Luke knew the Italian words for all the flavours of ice cream in Nonno's parlour, if only because he was rewarded for getting them right with a sweet sample.

Nonno was proud of Luke's effort and interest, especially since his son, Luke's Dad, had never tried to learn Italian, rebelling against his roots. He carried on teaching and encouraging Luke whilst raising him and his sister, Janine. Their mum had walked out on them when Luke was four, and they had moved in with Gran and Nonno because his Dad couldn't manage on his own.

Luke hadn't seen his mum ever since, but he didn't miss her much because he didn't really remember her, and besides, his Gran was always there for him. Sometimes he thought his Gran was better than a mum. Jamie and Chris's mums worked all day and they had to go to after-school clubs instead of getting to go home. Gran only worked mornings as a cleaner, so she was always around to spend time with Luke if he wanted. And she baked the best cakes.

Luke's Dad worked on a North Sea oil rig and so Luke went weeks at a time without seeing him. He did miss his Dad when he was away. Nonno was too old to play football and too scared to go on roller coasters, and neither grandparent could get into his RPG games on his Xbox. It wasn't like he had an uncle to do that sort of thing with him either. He only had an aunt, Francesca.

Aunt Fran worked with Nonno in the ice-cream parlour. She was okay though hot-tempered, but he only ever saw her at the shop. She hated coming to the house because Gran was always telling her to find someone to settle down with or it would be too late. Luke sympathised with Aunt Fran a bit there; Dad had tried to settle down and ended up alone anyway. And with 'responsibilities'.

Despite being confident of his ability to talk to his hosts, they were still complete strangers to him, and Luke was still away from home on his own for the first time. The Vallis were travelling on foot despite seeming to live some distance away from the town centre. In fact, all of the Micklemarsh pupils had left the square on foot or, if they were lucky, in a cart drawn by a horse or donkey.

'Does anyone have cars here?' Luke asked Riccardo.

'Some people do, though they don't use them much,' Riccardo explained. 'There aren't many roads and the few that we have are narrow and rough. Animals are much better at getting about on the tracks in these hills.'

'It's like being in the past,' Luke said.

They finally reached the Vallis' home; a single storey flat-roofed cottage built of rough stone.

'Don't you even have electricity here?' Luke exclaimed when they went inside to find Marcella's mum lighting oil lamps.

Riccardo laughed. 'The town has electricity, of course, but we don't have the money to pay for that expense. Oil lamps are just as good anyway.'

'But how will I charge my phone?' Luke asked, even more dismayed now he'd realised he couldn't do that. Surely people in Europe couldn't be this poor? He'd had no idea! He looked hard at Riccardo for the first time. He probably wasn't even forty but he looked twenty years older than that. He hunched his thin body over and pointed his head at the ground. His hair was greying and his face had heavy wrinkles of dejection. He had large black bags under eyes, which had a bleakness about them as well as a small flame of pride or resentment.

'There's no signal here so it'll be pretty useless. But if you need it, you'll just have to ask your friends,' Ricardo replied.

Marcella gave Luke a tour of her home. It didn't take long as the house was very small. Too small! It had only two bedrooms and so Luke had to share with

Marcella. One of the families involved in the exchange had suddenly moved out of Caravalla because of their failing vineyard, and the English pupils were already on their way. It meant numbers hadn't worked out and Luke had been the boy who had to share with a girl. He didn't mind too much since he was used to his sister, though she was two years older.

Luke and Marcella washed before dinner and joined the family at the centuries old farmhouse table. Marcella's mum, Serena, sat down, placing only a silver filigree basket of bread in the centre of the table. She wasn't like the other mothers Luke had seen in the town square. They had reminded him of his Gran, curvaceous and kind-looking. Marcella's mum was tall and thin, with a narrow, pale face. Her clothes were not exactly fashionable but there was something about the way she wore them that suggested she didn't belong in the country. She had only given Luke a cold acknowledgement when they had been introduced and hadn't spoken much to Riccardo or Marcella either.

It was Marcella who broke the silence, exclaiming 'Wow, this *is* a special occasion. The family silver only comes out for birthdays and Christmas.'

'Of course it's a special occasion,' Riccardo said. 'Luke it's an honour to have you in our humble home. Welcome!'

'Thanks,' Luke replied. He started to automatically say 'It's really lovely to be here', but without access to life's basics, he wasn't sure that it was and so couldn't bring himself to say so. He finished his sentence with 'lovely silver' instead, and immediately wondered how they could afford to buy, or at least to not sell, silver when they couldn't afford electricity.

He had just drawn breath and opened his mouth to wonder out loud when Riccardo responded: 'Thank you. No matter how bad things get, it's the one thing we can never part with. It's been passed down through the women in Serena's family for countless generations.'

'Wow, yeah, it has some serious sentimental value, then,' Luke said. He was genuinely in awe as his family didn't have anything like that. Nonno had settled in the U.K. with 'nothing but the shirt on his back', as he was fond of saying. Gran had some stuff of her own gran's kicking about, like a sewing machine that looked more like a mediaeval torture instrument, but none of the stuff was really that old.

'Oh, no, it's not that,' Riccardo said. 'There's an ancient curse on it, and anyone who possesses the silver who isn't a woman of Sorella blood will be doomed to a life of misery.'

Luke had to work hard to keep in a contemptuous snort of a giggle. As far as he could see, the Vallis had a pretty miserable existence despite having the silver.

'Anyway, enough about our family for now. Please, Luke, tuck in, and tell us about yourself.'

They poured olive oil and balsamic vinegar onto their plates from small silver jugs that had flip-tops and elegant slender spouts, and took slices of the aromatic fresh bread to dip in it.

'My name's Luke Silvester. I'm thirteen. I live in Micklemarsh with my grandparents, my Dad when he's not working away, and my sister, Janine. Janine's fifteen and a pain in the – err – my Gran's name is Bella, my Nonno's Giorgio and my Dad is Peter. I like football, reading and gaming. This is my first trip to Italy and I'm really excited about it 'cause my Nonno came from Naples. He changed his surname a bit when he moved to England, from Silvestre to Silvester. Um... that's it, I think.'

Luke wondered how his friends were coping with the language at their hosts' houses. He was sure they'd be managing this kind of small talk at least as it was one of the first things they'd learnt in class. And were Jamie and Chris only getting bread to eat too? Because the bread was gone, and now he'd finished speaking, no-one got up to fetch the next course. It didn't seem that this was a starter to the meal as Luke would have expected; it was the meal. His empty stomach growled in frustration.

'Now I'll tell you about me and my family,' Riccardo said. 'We are a small family, just me, Serena, and Marcella, who's eleven.' Serena tried to shrink back into the shadows when Riccardo mentioned her. She seemed to want Luke to see as little of her as possible. Maybe she was shy? But Luke felt that there was more to it than that. Serena seemed to be harbouring resentment towards him, but Luke couldn't think why. He had made sure to compliment her silverware, and couldn't think of anything he could have done to offend her in such a short time. The Vallis had volunteered to be hosts, and he was paying to stay there. Riccardo certainly seemed eager to have Luke there, chattering away about his family.

'We're just simple people, living simple lives. Not very interesting for you I'm afraid. And Marcella won't have much time to play because she has work to do. We all have to do our bit to scrape a living from our little farm.'

Luke wondered what bit Serena did since she didn't look as tanned and rugged from outdoor work as her daughter.

Luke felt like he might offend them all now with his next question, but he was starving. He couldn't believe that the bread was all they were getting.

'Will there be anything else to eat?'

'I'm sorry Luke, but as I've said, we're very poor, we can't afford a proper meal every day,' Riccardo said.

'Oh. Err... Well I think I'll go to bed now then.

I'm tired from all the travelling and I've got an early start tomorrow. We're having a picnic and finding out about wine making, so it'll be a busy day. Good night!'

Luke went to the bedroom, annoyed. He was contributing towards his stay after all, and he expected to at least be fed properly. He was very grateful that his Gran had supplied him with a decent stash of crisps and cakes.

'What have you got?' Marcella asked as she entered the bedroom, ready for bed.

'Nothing. Just crisps,' he said, as casually as he could. As if it wasn't bad enough that he had to share a bedroom, now it looked like he'd be asked to share his food too.

'Can I have some?' Marcella asked.

Luke wanted to say no. Why should he give anything to Marcella when her family was half-starving him? But his conscience pricked at him, telling him that it wasn't Marcella's fault and that she must be just as hungry as he was.

'Yeah, here,' Luke said, chucking Marcella a packet.

'Thanks, Luke,' Marcella said, catching and examining them. 'Wow, real English crisps! Cheese and onion, though?' She laughed and Luke couldn't help laughing with her, and he relaxed a bit.

'Would it be okay if I called you Marcy?' Luke asked. 'Marcella sounds too formal.'

'If you like,' Marcy said, shrugging. 'It makes me sound American and cool.'

They chatted about their lifestyles while they ate their secret feast, then settled down for the night. Luke thought that Marcy seemed mature for an eleven-year-old and supposed it must be because of the work she did and having no time for fun. She kind of looked older too, tall like her mum, and her skin was perhaps a bit weathered by her outdoor life. Yet she wore her long black hair tied in a tight, childish, plait, and her simple and worn-looking clothes made her seem younger than her years too. Luke was used to girls Marcy's age being dressed in the latest fashions and starting to wear make-up. Whatever, at least Marcy was friendly, unlike her weird mum.

Luke tried to stop thinking and start sleeping but he was too hyperactive. All he could see when he closed his eyes was a never-ending grey ribbon of road. Remembering his two days of boredom on the bus, Luke was reminded of Miss Trebor's story about the witch. If only magic were real, Luke thought. Then the Vallis could conjure up something for them all to eat. Was his entire stay going to be this bad?

2 AFTER DINNER GAMES

The class trudged round the rotten vineyards. They were supposed to be learning how wine was made but because there were no grapes that year they had to imagine all the processes that were being described.

'Borrrrring,' Jamie growled.

'At least I understand what's going on for once, though,' Chris muttered in reply. Miss Trebor was translating from their guide's Italian because the subject was too technical, even for Luke.

'No food, no drink,' Luke murmured.

'Eh?' Jamie asked.

'Oh, I was just thinking about last night. We got bread and water for dinner. Can you believe it? What did you have?'

'Normal stuff. Well, normal for here, I guess. Some kind of meat with potatoes and veg. Mmm, and there was pudding too. Fruit tart and custard. Didn't you see my Insta pics?'

'Sounds yum,' Luke sighed. 'No, no phone signal apparently.'

'Duh! Use the WiFi.'

'There isn't any. They don't even have electricity!'
'What?!'

'That reminds me, can I borrow your battery thing to charge my phone every day?'

'Whoa, your family sounds weird! Yeah, here,' Chris said, passing Luke his portable charger.

'Thanks. Yeah, or they're just bonkers. But Riccardo reckons it's all 'cause they're too poor,' Luke said.

'What? That's ridiculous.' Jamie exclaimed. 'The Moscaris told me the Vallis are the only family whose grapes haven't died for the past two years. How can they be poorer than everyone else? Or maybe I understood them wrong...'

'Now you mention it, Riccardo's vineyards did look all right. And they own silver baskets and jugs which they reckon isn't 'cos they're really rich, but because some dead witch'll curse them if they sell it, or something like that. Maybe this whole 'we're so poor' thing's just an act to make money out of my stay. I think I'll do a bit of fishing tonight,' Luke resolved.

Luke was served a sloppy stew that night. There was something chewy in it that might have been meat but was too unappetising to swallow.

Luke was tired of this game, if it was a game, and so decided to be brave and come right out with it. 'My friend said you've got the only vineyard not to have gone bad this year.'

Serena stiffened in her chair.

'Yes, it was the same last year too. It's very strange. And yet we're still poor,' Riccardo answered from beside his wife's intent stare. 'I just don't know where the money goes,' he explained. Serena dropped her eyes to the ground.

When the simple meal was over Marcy disappeared

without a word. Luke sat with Riccardo and Serena, uncomfortable in the silence. Riccardo read an Italian newspaper which was nearly a week old. Serena filed her nails. There was no TV, of course. Luke flicked through his gaming magazine which he had already read. The long journey had seen to it that he had already finished everything he had brought to keep himself occupied and now he was bored. He wondered where Marcy was. He drummed his fingers on the wooden arms of his tatty armchair. Was Marcy ever coming back?

'Where's Marcella gone?' he eventually asked. The sound of his own voice breaking the silence made him jump.

'Oh, I think she's just gone out for a walk,' Serena answered quickly. Luke thought it was rude of Marcy when she had a guest in need of entertaining. In fact, the whole family was just going on with their lives and completely ignoring him. For the first time in his life, Luke missed his cosy home and even his irritating sister. Whenever he was bored in Micklemarsh, he could always kick a ball about with the guys on the street. He wished he was back there now.

The next morning Luke asked Jamie what his hosts did with him in the evening.

'Um... Last night Josie and Adam and the families they're staying with came over and we played football in the field round the back. And on the first night we played hide and seek and watched TV.'

'Huh! All we did was sit in silence. Marcy went out, Serena was preening herself and Riccardo ended up doing his accounts. It was really boring,' Luke whinged.

'That sounds pretty bad,' Jamie sympathised.

'It wouldn't be as bad if they at least had a TV. Still, I don't suppose Italian TV's up to much?' Luke asked, hoping it was all melodramatic soaps.

'Actually, it's not too bad. They've got the usual stuff we watch, it's just all dubbed. Though you wouldn't have a problem. But then there was this clown show - it's a bit childish, but some of it was funny and 'cause it's slapstick it was really easy to follow. I think it's on again tonight; you should come over and watch it. In fact, come for dinner. The Moscaris always have lots of food so I'm sure they won't mind.'

'Thanks, but I don't think I can. Riccardo's house is miles from anywhere.'

'He must have a horse - borrow that. I'm sure he'll let you. I can draw you a map of how to get to the Moscaris' house from town.'

'Yeah, all right, I'll ask Riccardo. Thanks.'

That evening, having got grudging permission from Riccardo, Marcy took Luke to the barn and tacked up the donkey for him.

'Have you ridden before?' she asked Luke.

'Not really but I watch a lot of westerns,' he answered, thinking it looked pretty easy as long as you didn't lose your balance.

'Yeah, it's not hard, and for a donkey, Cico isn't too stubborn, he's too old for that. He should see you there and back without any trouble. Okay, there you go. Here's a torch, but don't come back too late. Apart from Dad going mad if you wake him, there are sometimes bandits about. Actually, let me check Dad's gun is in the case.'

'You have a gun?'

'Yeah, we all have them round here. I've been using it since I was about six.'

Although the thought of a gun excited Luke, it scared him more.

'Nah, you're all right. I don't know how to use a gun and someone might get hurt. Maybe I shouldn't

16

go...'

Luke's parents were always warning him and Janine not to go out alone at night in Micklemarsh. But it wasn't so dangerous that they felt they needed to carry a weapon to protect themselves. The last thing he expected to find in the Italian countryside was robbers. But then, a lot of the people here were poor and Luke understood how that might drive them to take desperate measures. He felt a shiver run down his spine.

'You'll be fine,' Marcy said. 'But you really should take the rifle. People always have one with them when they're out and about. That's why this is part of the tack.'

Marcy patted the wide and rigid leather tube that was strapped horizontally to the back of Cico's saddle. She unbuckled the cap that was at one end and half-pulled out a rifle.

'Actually, that's mostly to shoot anything tasty that crosses our path for dinner,' she continued. Luke thought about the suspicious chewy bits in last night's meal and then tried very hard to stop thinking about exactly what it was that had evidently crossed Riccardo's path yesterday.

Marcy continued: 'If you've never fired a gun, though, we should have a quick go. You like Xbox, you're gonna love this!'

Luke thought of his shoot-'em ups and started to share Marcy's enthusiasm.

Marcy accompanied Luke, who was astride Cico, as far as the main gate into the Vallis' property so the shots wouldn't disturb her dad' quiet time. She competently demonstrated how to use the gun, firing a couple of shots at a rusting bucket.

'Easy, see? You try.'

Luke tried. And missed. It wasn't as easy in real life as on the Xbox. And the butt kicking back into his shoulder wasn't much fun either.

'Yeah, easy for you with your years of practice. I'm so hopeless it wouldn't do me any good to have it.'

'No, you won't need to actually use it. You just show it to them before they get the better of you.'

Luke still wasn't sure.

'It'd just be easier if you came too. Nadia *is* your best friend,' he tried to persuade her.

'I really can't, I have to do my chores. But you have a good time, now.'

Luke did have a good time at the Moscaris'. After dinner they played games and then they watched the show that Jamie had told him about. It was on every Tuesday and Thursday at eight o'clock and was called "Ecco Enrico!" ("Here's Harry!"). Enrico was indeed a clown and like all clowns the things he did weren't particularly new or humorous.

Nadia and Elena, the Moscari children, were younger than the Micklemarshers and they laughed their heads off. Luke really liked one part of the show though, where Enrico brought on novelty animal acts: the singing dog and the assault course tortoise, which was especially funny because the footage had been speeded up as the tortoise was so slow.

After the show there was a boisterous discussion and re-enactment of the funniest bits, and the evening was rounded off by Luke and Jamie telling the family about their day visiting the villages further North in the mountains.

Then the Moscaris announced that they were going to bed. Luke looked at his watch. It was after ten. Luke wondered what time Marcy thought of as "late". Since everyone in the country went to bed early the roads would be creepily quiet by now.

Luke could feel his heart beat faster and he almost

asked Signor Moscari if he could stay the night. But Riccardo didn't have a telephone so there would be no way of letting the Vallis know and even though they ignored him when he was there, he was sure Riccardo and Marcy would worry about him if he wasn't. And Riccardo would go mad if the donkey wasn't back for work in the morning, and that was more certain and therefore scarier than the possibility of something happening on the way there. Plus he'd look totally pathetic if he was grown up enough to go on holiday without his family but too chicken to ride a couple of miles in the dusk.

Nadia came to the stable to help Luke tack up and mount the donkey, accompanied by Jamie with a carrot, curious as he had never seen a donkey.

'He's quite sweet, really,' Jamie said, patting Cico's furry neck. 'What's his name?'

'Cico,' Luke answered.

'Cheeko? Like cheeky?'

'Something like that,' Luke was too tired to remind Jamie of the rules of Italian pronunciation.

'He looks a bit too past-it to be cheeky to me,' Jamie said. 'See ya tomorrow then.'

Luke set off into the darkening night. It was lucky that the donkey knew his way home as it was difficult to see where he was going on the unlit road. The torchlight was as stingy as everything else in the Vallis' house and was only good for picking out the big stones and potholes that he needed to steer Cico round.

As Luke reached the gate on the perimeter of Riccardo's property he could make out a figure hanging onto the bars of the gate. Luke immediately thought it must be a thief trying to break in, and his heart started pounding and his legs felt weak.

He eventually commandeered his rebellious legs and

kicked his instructions to the donkey to turn and go but Cico refused to retrace his steps now he was almost home. Luke then realised there was nowhere to go anyway. There were no hiding places nearby, and if he went for help, by the time anyone got here the robber would have long since vanished with the Vallis' only possession worth taking; the silverware which they kept on a dresser right by the door.

Besides, it wasn't very fair of him to leave the Vallis at the mercy of the burglar. Especially when he had their gun. Hey, yeah, the gun! Luke would have to show he was boss, like Marcy said, and scare the robber off.

'Hey, you!' Luke's voice trembled as he shouted at the figure.

The man didn't turn around.

Luke unbuckled the gun from behind him and carefully lifted it out of its case.

'I'm warning you to go! I've got a gun!'

The burglar still took no notice of Luke, just persisted in his attempts to get over the gate. He wasn't getting far though. It looked like he might have got caught on something. Luke wasn't taking any chances by getting any nearer, so he repeated his warning and cocked the gun like Marcy had showed him.

When he still didn't get a response Luke thought the robber must be hard of hearing. He got off Cico in case the sound of the gun scared him, pointed the rifle into the air, squeezed his eyes shut and fired it. Despite being prepared for how it would sound and feel from his trial earlier, he still jumped violently. Cico didn't seem to have batted an eyelid.

Astonishingly, the threat had no effect on the burglar either!

'He must be really nasty. He'd probably think nothing of murdering the Vallis in their sleep before stealing all their things. I have to stop him while I still have the chance.'

With adrenaline pumping through his system, he mustered all his gaming experience and aimed the gun at the bandit's legs this time. Luke fired and the man fell to the ground. Luke shakily opened the gate, not daring to look at what he had just done. He felt suddenly overwhelmed by the consequences of his half-thinking actions, and followed Cico's charge right past the man and on into the safety of Riccardo's house.

Marcy was awake and upright in bed when Luke burst, panting, into the bedroom.

'Are you all right?' she asked him.

'No! You know those bandits you told me about? Well I just found one trying to break into your house!'

'What?' Marcy asked, her jaw dropping in horror.

'He was trying to climb over the gate, but he was stuck on something. And he wouldn't go when I warned him so I shot him!'

'On the gate?' Marcy asked, looking more relaxed now.

'Yes! Go wake your dad and get him to go and have a look. I only wanted to shoot him in the leg, but I may have got him somewhere more serious.'

'Don't worry. I've a feeling everything's fine,' Marcy said, unable to suppress a mischievous smile.

'What do you mean, "Don't worry"?'

'Let's go and have a look ourselves first.'

'But it could be dangerous.'

'You're the dangerous one!' Marcy said, giggling now. 'Come on.'

They set off outside, carrying on their conversation in whispers until they were well clear of the house.

'I don't know why you're finding this so funny,' Luke hissed. 'I'm in big trouble.' He swore then with a new realisation. 'I could be a murderer!'

Marcy burst out laughing.

'Shut up!' Luke screeched.

'Or what?' she retorted. 'You'll shoot me too?' Marcy was laughing so hard she had to stop walking to catch her breath.

Luke had never felt so terrified and guilty in his life. And Marcy's bizarre reaction was just making things worse. Was she nuts?

'Marcy, please! This is serious.' Luke had to stop now. They were near the gate.

'God, Luke,' said Marcy, suddenly straight faced when she saw the immobile shape on the ground by the gate. 'What have you done? Such a senseless waste!' but then she was laughing again.

'Stop laughing!' Luke cried at her from his position further back.

'Oh, come here,' Marcy said, coaxingly.

'No way.'

'Really. I think you should come and have a proper look.'

'Just tell me if it's bad.'

'No, it's not. It's a pretty good shot this time. Oh, it's not fair to tease anymore! Luke, you haven't hurt anyone. Have a look.'

Luke started forward but on seeing the crumpled form, he stopped and turned his face away.

'Really, it's okay,' Marcy said and Luke, reassured by her calmer attitude and the fact that she wasn't screaming like a girl from a horror film, finally faced up to his actions.

Instead of a slain man he found a sheepskin rug. 'What?' he cried, looking at Marcy with his eyes bulging in disbelief. Marcy shrugged. Luke turned back to the rug and saw that it was pierced with a bullet-hole. 'But...?'

Marcy tugged at his arm, gently pulling him away

from the rug and back towards the house. 'Luke, it was just a sheepskin we … hang on the gates at night to scare away bad spirits. You didn't really think it was a person did you?'

'Yes!' Luke said, exasperated. 'It was dark; it really looked like a person when it moved in the wind…' But Luke couldn't feel any breeze and he was sure there hadn't been one five minutes ago either. He was too angry to give the phenomenon much thought, though. 'You could have told me before instead of letting me think I'd hurt someone!' he scolded Marcy.

'I suppose so,' Marcy said soberly. 'Sorry Luke, it just seemed so funny I couldn't help playing along.'

'Well it *wasn't* funny.' Luke retorted and stomped off to bed, leaving Marcy to untack Cico who'd made it through the open stable door to his hay manger. Luke had had enough dealings with the Vallis for one day; be they two-legged, four-legged, or no-legged.

Luke was still in a bad mood when he woke up the next day.

'What's wrong with you?' Jamie asked him when they boarded the bus for their day trip to Florence.

'That stupid Marcy! She played a really horrible trick on me last night.'

'Yeah? What did she do?'

'She told me this stupid scare story about robbers prowling the area and how I shouldn't stay out at yours too late. She even gave me a loaded gun to protect myself!'

'What?' Jamie exclaimed, incredulous. 'You never told me! You could have shown me!'

'I'd totally forgotten I had it while I was with you guys. Anyway, while I was gone, Marcy hung a sheepskin on the gate and it was so dark when I got back that I thought it was a thief trying to get in and I shot at it.'

Instead of meeting with the expected sympathy, his story provoked a burst of laughter from his best friend.

'Oh yeah, ha ha!' Luke growled.

'What's so funny?' Chris asked, leaning over from the seat behind.

'Luke was attacked by a rug and he shot it in self-defence!' Jamie scoffed.

'What?' Chris asked, and without fully understanding he laughed along with Jamie all the same.

'Oh, not you too,' Luke grumbled at Chris. 'Marcy thought it was hilarious as well. But *I* thought I'd really hurt someone! She's such a –'

'But how could you mistake a rug for a person?' Jamie butted in.

'That's the weird thing. It was moving around, like it was trying to get over her gate but I can't see how. There wasn't any wind.'

'Oo-oo-oo, must have been a ghost!' Chris mocked.

'Or Arianna's witchcraft,' Jamie suggested.

'Or maybe Luke's just a big chicken. Buck-buck-buck-aw!' Chris shrilled and turned round to share the fun.

Luke folded his arms and knotted his eyebrows. Great! Marcy's bad joke had just got worse. It spread like a wildfire along the bus and now Luke would never hear the end of it. He wished he'd never come on this stupid trip.

The dull traipsing round the pointless old art of the packed Uffizi gallery didn't help anyone forget about Luke's escapade last night, but he felt avenged whenever his classmates got told off for being too noisy every time they made fun of him. The boat trip along the river shut everyone up, though. The higgledy-piggledy mediaeval buildings spread along the banks were an amazing sight. They had even sprouted up on the bridges.

But back on the bus, Chris and Jamie sat together leaving Luke stewing on his own. His story was laughingly exaggerated and tossed back and forth so that Luke arrived back in Caravalla in as foul a mood as ever. Marcy met him off the bus to walk him home, and kept asking questions about his day but he steadfastly ignored her.

He ate the evening meal – a fairly satisfying slice of turkey with potatoes – without saying much, answering the Vallis' questions about his day in grunts. When he had finished eating he promptly excused himself, saying he was tired and going to bed. Once he had finished in the bathroom he found Marcy was waiting for him in the bedroom.

'Luke,' she began.

'Just go away!' he protested. 'I don't want to speak to you!'

'I was just going to tell you what really happened!' Marcy whined back.

'What do you mean?'

'Well, you thought that rug was a person didn't you? You said it was because it was moving in the wind.'

'Yes,' Luke said sharply, bracing himself for more teasing.

'But it wasn't a windy night.'

'No, that was weird. But I don't care! This is a stupid town with stupid people and stupid rugs, and I just want to get out of here.' Luke wondered if it really was possible to go home right now, or even stay with a different family.

'But I want to explain,' Marcy insisted. 'I feel so guilty and I don't want you to fall out with me. Though it was my fault.'

'Yeah, I know whose fault it was, thanks!'

'But you don't know it's because my mum's a witch

and I messed up one of her spells.'

'Oh, grow up, Marcy.' Luke said after a stunned pause. He certainly hadn't been expecting that as an excuse.

'It's true! I know it's hard to believe. I didn't believe it either when she first told me. I help her collect the ingredients so that people don't get suspicious of her. That's where I keep disappearing to in the evenings. People round here are superstitious, and really quick to suspect witchcraft. That's why she's so annoyed about having you stay here in case you found out.'

'So what magic does she do?' asked Luke. How far was Marcy going to take this?

'I don't really know. Last night she sent me for a handful of wool from one of our neighbour's sheep but Arturo was in the field checking them over. I knew Mum'd go ballistic if I went home empty-handed so I walked past the rug-maker's workshop and grabbed some wool from one of the sheepskins drying outside instead.

'Mum wouldn't let me watch what she did with it so I secretly followed her onto our roof and hid behind the rainwater tank. She cast a spell to make the sheep whose wool it was come to our house. I went to bed then so she wouldn't catch me spying.

'Because I had taken the wool from a rug instead of a sheep, the spell worked on the rug and made it come to life and come here. I suppose you were a bit freaked out by the things I'd said about the bandits so when you saw the rug trying to get in you mistook it for a thief. I'm really sorry.'

Luke knew that there had certainly been something unnatural about that rug. But witchcraft? That was ridiculous. Marcy must have heard the taunts of his classmates as they were getting off the bus that evening and was trying to drag him further into her embarrassing jokes. He wondered why she was being so nasty. Perhaps it was because she was an only child and was trying to play some sort of game with him.

'Please don't tell anyone, though,' she wheedled. 'If people find out, they'll turn against us and Mum might even get put in jail, even though she only does good magic. I only told you because I felt I owed you an explanation for last night. Promise not to tell?'

'What's the point? It's all just rubbish,' he told her.

'No it's not. I can show you her spell book and ingredients.'

'Oh, yeah, like bottles of spiders' legs are concrete evidence. Good night.'

He blew out the lantern and lay back and closed his eyes, not sure he'd sleep as he was so angry. Then he thought he could hear something odd, but it was probably just Marcy settling down. No! There it was again. A scrabbling sound on the wooden floor. Luke felt an approaching feeling of disgust. He fumbled for the matches and lit the lamp, hoping that it wasn't. But it was. There was a mouse pattering across the floor.

'What's up?' Marcy asked, blinking a bit in the gentle light.

'Eugh! It's a mouse!' Luke cried.

'Oh, they're all right. We get them all the time,' Marcy said simply. 'Go back to sleep.'

'No way, not with that in here. I'm not having it crawl on me in the night. It might gnaw my ears or something!'

'Yeah, I guess it wouldn't have a problem finding them, since they're so big.'

'Oh, shut up and get rid of it.'

'You get rid of it; you're the one bothered by it.'

Luke got out of bed and grabbed the only thing he had to hand; his hefty gaming magazine. Then he prowled after the mouse which was making shaky progress. He seized his chance and whacked at the floor. Luke didn't expect to be fast enough to hit it and so was surprised to have caught its tail. Perhaps it was ill? It certainly wasn't well now that Luke had practically amputated its tail and it squeaked a disturbingly human scream. Luke instantly took pity on the poor little thing and lifted off his magazine and the terrified creature hobbled out of the room through the gap under the door.

'See? It was going anyway. You're so cruel,' Marcy scolded him.

Luke did feel a bit cruel now, but he justified it to himself and Marcy: 'It was self-preservation. Anyway, I don't know what you're so worried about. Mice are bad for farms, eating your crops and grain stores.'

'Yes, but there's more humane ways of killing them than boring them to death with a games magazine,' Marcy sniped.

'What like casting little spells on them and asking them to move somewhere else?' Luke retorted and huffed the lamp out. He listened carefully in the darkness for the return of the mouse or any of its sharp-toothed friends coming to wreak revenge, but there was no sound in the pitch black. His thoughts turned to Serena. She couldn't be a witch! But there was definitely something odd about her. Chris and Jamie's taunting comments about Arianna the witch echoed round his head. But that was just idle teasing…

3 TRANSFORMATIONS

'Any more witchly goings-on to report?' asked Chris on the bus on the way to Pisa the next day.

Luke was sitting next to Chris today and Jamie was on the seat in front with Adam. He turned round to take part in this conversation though. Luke decided not to tell his friends Marcy's insistence that her mum was a witch. It would only lead to being picked on again, one way or another.

'Yeah, right. Biggest excitement was a mouse in the bedroom,' Luke said.

'Aww, did it scare you?' Chris mocked.

'No, actually, I chopped its tail off with my mag,' Luke boasted.

'Yeah? There is a reason for making games mags that thick then,' Jamie joked, and all three of them shared a friendly laugh. It looked like Luke was in for a better day than yesterday, then, though he still hadn't forgiven Marcy for her humiliating joke.

'Serena was acting a bit weird this morning though. She was much more mumsy, running around after us all.'

'Maybe she's realised what a cow she was being,' Jamie suggested.

'Nah, it was more like she didn't want to sit down.'

'She must have a sore bum. Maybe it's piles!' They all laughed at Chris's joke.

'She's been fine all week though. Whatever's wrong with her has happened suddenly,' Luke puzzled.

'Well that proves it then.' Chris said. 'She really is a witch and she turned herself into that mouse you had a go at. Ha ha ha!'

'No, 'cause then her whole bum'd be missing,' Jamie chimed in.

Luke reflected on his lie that he had taken the mouse's tail right off.

The leaning tower of Pisa was, well, leaning, and the rest of the sights consisted of more buildings and artwork. Luke was relieved that they only had one more day in Italy before setting off for home. The holiday hadn't been much of an adventure at all, and the most interesting things that had happened had been scary and unpleasant. He just had to get through a boring Sunday stuck in Caravalla and then he would be homeward bound. Since he didn't have much longer with the Vallis, he decided to broach the subject of witchcraft that evening. He wondered what kind of reaction it would provoke.

'Riccardo,' Luke said at dinner. 'Do you know any witch stories?' The out-of-the-blue question was a like a hot poker to Serena's already problematic bottom as she straightened her stance. 'Miss Trebor told us one about a witch called Arianna in Florence.'

'Yes, I know that story too. Serena is from Florence and her father told me the tale one day. But it happened a long time ago. Anyway, enough of this. It is not good to talk of the black arts. You never know what might hear you and curse you for it.' Riccardo looked anxiously about him and shuddered.

But Luke wasn't letting him get out of talking about the subject that easily. 'Well, that story got my friends' minds working overtime. You'll laugh at this; they think you're a wizard who's been blighting everyone else's crops to put them out of business so that you can buy their farms up cheap and get rich.'

'What a silly idea! I don't have any money to buy anything!' Riccardo protested, but there was a droplet or two of sweat on his brow now. It suddenly occurred to Luke that rather than accusing Riccardo to deflect attention from Serena, he had actually hit the nail on the head.

'Oh, they think that really you're rich and are just pretending to be poor to hide what you're up to.'

'That's ridiculous! If I had money, I would spend it on food and electricity, on nice clothes for my wife and games for my daughter,' Riccardo stated angrily.

'Please don't be mad, they're just having fun,' Luke apologised. 'We don't even believe in magic.'

'You may not, but in Caravalla we do, and it is not a game. People here are already suspicious of us because we are the only ones not cursed by this blight on the vineyards. You and your friends are only adding fuel to their fire. Please stop!'

'Okay, okay, we won't talk about it anymore!' Luke said. But he thought much more about it. So everyone in Caravalla suspected that the Vallis were up to something, and now Luke was inclined to agree with them. Riccardo was anxious to quell Luke's friends' jokes so as not to draw more attention to his family. And Marcy had been right that Serena resented Luke being there because he might find out what they were up to. But it was too late because he had already guessed it and it wasn't magic. They were spraying everyone else's crops with something to make them rot. And it was most likely a substance that Serena brewed herself, out of sight on her roof, making Marcy think she was conjuring potions.

When they had finished eating, Serena excused herself, saying she had a headache and needed some fresh air. Marcy looked pointedly at Luke with a 'told you so' expression on her face. Luke retaliated with a raised-eyebrow look that said 'uh-huh'. They rose from their seats as one and went up to Marcy's room to continue the discussion verbally.

'Bet you she's doing magic,' Marcy hissed as soon as the door was shut.

'Bet *you* she's not,' Luke said. 'She's making poison, not potion, Marcy. She sprays it on your neighbours' crops at night.'

'Do you really think she *is* poisoning their crops? She promised me she wasn't doing anyone any harm. I'm scared enough she's going to get caught but if she's doing *that*…'

'Marcy, it's not magic, just chemistry. But I can see how you'd be fooled into thinking –'

'I may be younger than you but I'm not stupid!' Marcy butted in. 'Chemistry doesn't need spells! Come on, let's go up on the roof now and spy on her and maybe you'll see something that science can't explain.'

Marcy led him silently up the steep wooden stairs and through a door onto the flat roof where Serena had crept earlier after making a show of going out the front door. Luke and Marcy hid behind an enormous tank that caught rainwater. Serena was facing the moon, standing in front of a trestle table laid with a lit candle, a small sack, three bowls and three small bottles. One bottle was full and stoppered with a cork, and two were empty, their stoppers lying patiently at the base of their masters. Serena did indeed appear to be casting a spell but Luke held firm to his theory. 'So the recipe for the poison is hundreds of years old and has lots of dusty belief attached,' he thought. 'The results are the same in the end, words or no words.'

Serena poured some of the contents of the bowl she had been chanting over into an empty bottle and then began working with a new bowl. Into it she poured something that looked like water. Into the water she poured powder from another bottle, and stirred the two together with a bird's feather, chanting:

> 'I call on the powers of Hecate
> To grant unto me through this bowl
> A magic drink which, consumed by me,
> Will make me turn into an owl.'

Marcy provided a hushed commentary: 'I think she wants to be an owl so that she can do whatever she's going to do with those other potions without being suspected.'

'People can't turn into animals, Marcy.'

'Maybe not with chemistry. You'll see.'

Luke had to admit that the concept, though ridiculous, was exciting. Wouldn't it be fantastic to be a bird?

Serena blew out the candle and then did something Luke hadn't expected. She drank some of her latest poison from the bowl! Luke watched with his heart in his mouth, waiting for her to drop down dead. Nothing seemed to happen until Luke suddenly realised that Serena's mouth had turned into a beak.

He thought he must be seeing things and squeezed his eyelids together in a hard blink. When he opened his eyes he saw the toenails on Serena's bare feet had turned into talons. And now the skin on her face and arms was sprouting feathers. It was freakish to look at, almost too horrible. Too wrong. Too unreal!

Luke shuddered and looked at Marcy. Her excited face was confirmation that it wasn't just him imagining this. Her mouth took a split-second break from its delighted grin to shape the word 'see?'.

But Luke couldn't get his head around what seemed to be happening. It just wasn't possible! He stared at Marcy, his eyebrows crumpled with the effort of forcing his brain to reason things through. His mouth kept forming questions that got no further than 'wha…' or 'how…', making Marcy clasp a hand over her mouth to stifle a giggle.

'You look like a goldfish,' she hissed, mimicking his circular mouth opening and closing. Then she nodded her head urgently towards her mum to direct his attention back to the action.

The transformation continued, regardless of Luke's incredulity. Serena's arms became wider and were suddenly wings and her whole body shrank until it was the size of an owl.

Serena-the-owl stepped out of her crumpled clothes and hopped onto the table to pick up a bottle of potion in her beak. She grabbed a second bottle in her claws, along with the sack. Then she test-flapped her wings and took off, rather unsteadily, into the night.

Serena's lack of grace triggered a memory of the rickety action of the mouse that Luke had walloped the night before. Luke's brain began to reboot as he realised that the mouse had been Serena, probably spying on Marcy to see if she was giving away her secret.

Luke and Marcy stood up out of their crouch.

'See? See? I told you!' Marcy cried, but Luke wasn't really listening.

He stared off into the night sky in the direction Serena had flown. His mind was working overtime now, his heart pumping powerfully as he imagined the sensation of soaring through the air as a wild and cunning bird of prey, scouring the visible darkness below for the minute movements of a meal. The strength of his desire broke the statue-spell upon him and he ran to the table and grabbed the nearest bowl.

'What are you doing?' Marcy shrilled.

'That was amazing! I want to try it.'

'No! We need to get out of here before Mum gets back and catches us.'

'She's just left! She won't be back for ages. I can become an owl too and follow her to find out what she's doing,' Luke said.

'Wait! I don't think –' Marcy said, running towards him as he guzzled down the remnants of the solution in the bowl.

'– I don't think that bowl was the one with the owl potion in,' Marcy finished, too late.

Luke belched, discarded the bowl and Marcy's comment, and started flapping his gangly arms in preparation. But instead of growing feathers, Luke's skin was sprouting hair.

'Oh, Luke!' Marcy said crossly, folding her arms and drumming her fingers on her elbow whilst she watched what happened next.

Luke found he was losing the ability to move his fingers, and when he looked at his hand, it was becoming a hoof. His silver ring was pushed off his little finger and spun, tinkling, on the ground.

'Umm…' he said.

He lifted his foot and his trainer fell off. When he stamped his foot back down it made a dull 'clop' and had also become a hoof. He felt a tail grow from the end of his spine. His light brown hair grew down his lengthening neck and became an odd-looking mane with its coating of hair gel. His face stretched, his mouth felt enlarged and rubbery, his nostrils grew elongated and his ears reached for the sky. He opened his mouth to tell Marcy 'I think I've been turned into a horse!' but all that came out was 'Ee-orr! Ee-orr!'.

It was worse than being a horse.

'Yes, you're a donkey, Luke, well done!' Marcy said examining the objects on the table. 'This was the bowl with the owl potion in,' Marcy said, lifting the correct one off the table. 'And this must be the one that she made the antidote in. Drat! It's empty. I'm going to have to look through Mum's spell book and try to make a new antidote before she comes back and catches us or she'll go mad! And I'd better put you in the barn so that Dad – or anyone else – doesn't see a donkey on our roof. Come on!'

Luke found negotiating the stairs a difficult task since he now had four legs to coordinate. Fortunately, Riccardo had fallen into his usual deep sleep of exhaustion and wasn't disturbed by Luke's unshod hooves skidding and tripping down the narrow stairway. His broad flank dragged along both sides of the wall, leaving tufts of his new hair on the rough plaster. He was quite glad to get into the barn with its level, gripping, surface, and the straw cushioning of the donkey stall within.

'Right. I'll be back down as soon as I've made the antidote okay? Nod your head,' Marcy instructed. Luke nodded his head miserably. 'Oh cheer up! I'll soon get you sorted out. Look on the bright side: at least you're not so spotty!' Luke managed to bare his teeth at her but Marcy was already bustling off, padlocking the barn door behind her.

Back on the roof Marcy found a large bag on the floor which contained Serena's spell book and bottles. She flicked through the pages of the book and found the "Antidote for Metamorphosis".

"Required:
1 original hair or flake of skin etc.
1 tsp of essence of pupae
Water as required for desired viscosity
   Beneath the light of the moon, light a candle while saying *"This is the power of Hecate". Mix the ingredients together using a body part of the original animal while chanting:*
   "I call on the powers of Hecate
       To conjure a potion of form
       That when swallowed, the consumer shall be
       Returned to the shape it was born."
   Blow out the candle and the potion is ready. Half the quantity made will be sufficient for smaller animals, but larger animals are recommended to drink it in its entirety.
   NB The potion must be administered within 24 hours otherwise it will lose its effect."

Marcy searched through Serena's bottles for the Essence of Pupae. She was amused by the actual modesty of magic. It was nothing like the usual representation. There was no need for a vast room lined with shelves of innumerable spell books and bottles of gruesome beastie bits to plop into the massive cauldron bubbling over a fire. The only flame needed was a candle, and the only receptacle was a bowl or two. The amount of ingredients depended on the variety of magic you did. So simple, really. But Marcy supposed that the lightning and exotic ingredients of legend made magic seem more impressive and out of the reach of ordinary people.

Serena had told Marcy that magic was actually based on very simple rules. You couldn't make anything that didn't exist, and you couldn't make something from nothing. What you could do was control and change living things. You could turn one thing into another as long as it was similar in essence, such as animals with the same number of limbs. And you could influence the actions, ability and health of living things. But you couldn't conjure money or turn one pizza into two.

Marcy sneaked down to her bedroom to get a hair off Luke's pillow, and a clean bowl. Back on the roof she added a teaspoon of Essence of Pupae to the hair in the bowl. The essence was cremated caterpillar cocoons, from the stage where they are transforming into butterflies, and so was the catalyst for any kind of metamorphosis spell. She added the water and stirred the concoction with a very handy human body part: her finger.

That was all there was to it, thank goodness. Luke would be his old self in no time, and her mum need never know.

Luke had been left in the company of Riccardo's donkey, Cico. Cico didn't take as kindly to Luke now he was no longer human, afraid that Luke was after his hay so he turned his back end on Luke and threw out warning kicks. Luke had to press himself uncomfortably into a corner of the stall in order to keep well out of his way. He couldn't believe his bad luck. Instead of enjoying the fantastic freedom of an owl, he was trapped in the body of a donkey, stupid, heavy and hated. He was a great big joke. Again!

He hung his head in misery but he flung it up and pricked his ears along with Cico at the sound of strange noises at the gate. Footsteps passed the barn and then Riccardo's unlocked front door was opened and Luke could hear Riccardo shouting: 'Help! Thieves! Help!'. Luke didn't think it would do Riccardo much good given the isolation of his farm. There was a thump, followed by a thud, followed by silence from Riccardo. With his rotating donkey ears Luke could pick up the sound of the thieves scuffling around the house, robbing Riccardo of his belongings. He hoped that Riccardo and Marcy were all right.

The thieves left the house but to Luke's alarm headed straight for the barn and kicked the rickety old doors open. The thieves were disappointed to find only two donkeys, but one of them said "Sbetter'n nofink'.

Luke wondered what was better than nothing. The thieves went into the storeroom to fetch the tack. Luke couldn't believe the cheek of it; they were going to steal Riccardo's donkey to carry away his property!

'Wot? There's only one saddle! You'll just 'ave to go bareback Valentino.'

'Why would they need two? ... Oh no! They want to take me too,' Luke panicked. 'Well, just let them try,' he resolved. There was no way he was being taken away from that potion Marcy was making.

The bossy thief entered the stall and took a good look at both donkeys. 'You look the best of a bad pair,' he said to Luke and came forward to saddle him up. Luke moved away from him, but with two donkeys and two men in the stall, there wasn't much room for a chase, and Luke still hadn't quite got the hang of having four legs.

Cico carried on eating, much to Luke's frustration. 'Why can't he understand and help me dodge the thieves?' Luke thought. He resorted to turning his back on the men as Cico had done with him, to buck and kick, but the time he had figured out it was like trying to do a hand stand, the bossy robber had grabbed Luke's tufty forelock to force the bridle on him.

'Ow!' Luke tried to say, but all that came out was another bray. His head hurt where his hair had been pulled, and his tongue burned from the cold metal bit that was now fastened in his mouth. It tasted horrible, like sucking on tin foil. It hurt too when the thief yanked on the reins to force Luke to submit to the saddle.

The thief got on, his sack of silverware clanging against Luke's side. Luke felt that all was lost. There was no way he could get the hang of bucking with that lump on him. He had no choice but to join Cico's shaky progress onto the road. 'I'm being kidnapped,' Luke thought. 'How on earth will Marcy find me to give me the potion?'

4 DONKEYNAPPED

Marcy had escaped the thieves' attention by being on the roof, but they didn't escape hers. She watched dejectedly as the thieves left with Luke, the completed and now useless potion in her hand. When they were out of sight she rushed downstairs to see if her dad was all right. Riccardo had been hit on the head and was just beginning to come round.

'Oh, my head!' he groaned when he opened his eyes in his throbbing head. 'Why me? I have nothing! What did they even take?' he asked, looking around whilst delicately rubbing his lump. He saw Serena's family silver was gone from the dresser but otherwise things were much the same because they had nothing else worth taking. Marcy ignored his moans and asked the most important question: 'Are you all right, Dad?'

'I suppose so. How about you?'

'I'm fine. We could hear them from my bedroom so we jumped out of the window and hid.'

'Oh, good. Where's Luke now? And is Mum back from her walk yet?'

'I - I don't know where they are,' Marcy stuttered.

'Luke and I split up to hide.'

'Give them a shout for me, would you? My head hurts too much to do it myself.'

'Luke! Mum!' Marcy shouted half-heartedly. There was, of course, no answer.

'Try again. Shout louder. Tell them it's safe to come out now.'

Marcy did so but no one emerged.

'Mum must still be out, but where's Luke? God forbid anything's happened to a child entrusted to our care!' Riccardo squealed, the pitch of his voice rising in panic.

They searched the house in vain until they heard the front door close. Riccardo dashed into the hall to find Serena, who had just got home.

'Are you all right?' Riccardo asked, rushing to her.

'Yes,' Serena said, taken aback by Riccardo's excessive concern. 'Much better now, thanks. And I've got a surprise for you. I knitted some jumpers for a family over the hill; I don't think you know them. Anyway, they didn't have any cash to pay me so they gave me a donkey they don't need anymore. It's tied up outside. Isn't it perfect? With poor old Cico getting on a bit, and you worrying about how we could afford a new one? Where is Cico by the way? And what's happened to the barn door?'

'Is Luke with you?'

'No. Why should he be? Is that all the thanks I get? And where's my mother's coffee pot?' Serena asked, noticing the bare table.

'Gone! All your things are gone! It's dreadful! Terrible! How will we ever get it all back? I can't afford to replace it. What a cursed life!' Riccardo spluttered.

'What?'

'We've been burgled,' Marcy managed to explain, despite feeling disconcerted about the new donkey. She reckoned her mum had transformed one of Arturo's sheep with the donkey potion that Luke had drunk the remnants of. Then she must have drunk from the second bottle she took with her to turn back into a human and lead the donkey home. She must have had spare clothes in the sack she took.

'Oh no, how awful! That's why the barn door's smashed in and Cico's gone?'

'I think they've taken Luke too!' Riccardo wailed.

'Oh, don't be silly, darling! What would thieves want with Luke? He's probably just hiding somewhere. I'll go and get help while you two look for him in the outhouses and fields.'

As soon as they were alerted to Luke's absence, the townsfolk came out in force to find him. Luke's teachers and classmates helped everyone search their property. But no one could find Luke so the local police could only conclude that Luke had indeed been abducted by the burglars.

Marcy knew that Luke had indeed been taken by the thieves, but he had been donkeynapped rather than kidnapped and she didn't dare disclose the truth. But how would Luke ever be found if the police were looking for a boy?

'So are these imbeciles going to hold Luke to ransom then?' Riccardo asked the police. 'I have nothing else. They took everything of any value!'

'I think they probably took him as insurance against being caught. They'll probably let him go when they've got far enough away. He'll turn up in a day or two, you'll see. Meantime, we'll keep a look out and spread the word round the neighbouring villages.'

Luke's family was notified, and with nothing else to be done that night, the villagers sullenly traipsed off to bed.

Riccardo couldn't sleep. He fretted about how devastated Luke's family would be. Nothing ever went right for him. They were always poor no matter how well the farm seemed to do, and now they had lost the few precious things they had, including their honoured guest.

Serena lay awake brooding about the loss of her only nice things too. They had been in her family for years, passed down from generation to generation. Her sister, Anna, had never wanted Serena to inherit them in the first place because she had been worried about their safety on a farm, and now she had been proved right. If only she could turn back into an owl and fly off in search of the men, but with all the attention on their house now it was too risky.

Marcy couldn't sleep either. She didn't know what she was going to do. She felt awful about Luke. He must be going through hell. Not only was he suffering with being a donkey but he had been taken by bad men and was headed to who knows where. Even if he escaped, he probably wouldn't find his way to Caravalla to be turned back into a boy. She might never see him again.

Marcy was the only one who knew what had happened, and the only one who could possibly help, but she didn't see what she could do that would be of any use.

Her mum was the only person Marcy could tell; otherwise they would both get into a lot of trouble. But her mum was already angry and ashamed that Luke had gone missing while under her care and she would be furious if she found out they had been playing with magic. Marcy had only just been in trouble for the first time in her life, for messing up the sheep spell. She didn't want to own up to having done wrong again. She decided it would be okay to leave things for a couple of days – like the police said – in the hope that Luke made it back to Caravalla so that she could put it right without anyone ever knowing the truth.

Luke was really beginning to understand what Riccardo had meant about the toughness of the terrain. The thieves, afraid of capture, avoided what were considered to be main roads so Luke found himself stumbling over steep fields, forced to carry his heavy rider on his new legs right through the night.

At dawn they passed through a village and Luke tried desperately to alert the villagers. He tried to shout 'Help, help!' but all that came out was 'Hey-ha Hey-ha' and his rider whacked him with a stick for making such a racket.

With the daylight, Luke was able to get a proper look at his two captors. They were both rugged and filthy but were dressed in surprisingly decent clothes. They must literally rob the shirts off people's backs, Luke thought, hating the men even more. His newly acute sense of smell didn't like the pair much either.

The man on his back seemed to be in charge and was called Dino. Out of the corner of his rolling eyes, Luke could see Dino was a cliché of a bandit; short, swarthy and stubbly. The uneven lengths of his hair looked as though it had been cut with a knife. His chubby face was tanned, covered in rough stubble, and he had tiny black eyes which glinted darkly in the light. He wore once-cream chinos and a mostly-white shirt, with the sleeves rolled up to display blurry green tattoos up his forearms.

The robber astride Cico was Valentino, who was quite a contrast to Dino. As his name suggested, he was young and tall and handsome with long waves of hair, which he frequently swept back with a vain hand. He had grown a sculpted beard although it needed trimming. His clothes were similar to his companion's, but looser and flowing. Luke, sweating heavily beneath his hairy hide, eyed the cool garments with envy.

The thieves eventually stopped at a farm in order to get something to eat. Judging by the banter between the farmer and the thieves they were obviously old friends. The thieves gave the farmer something from the pack tied to Luke's saddle in exchange for food and the farmer's silence.

Luke and Cico were untacked and released into a paddock. Cico quickly got his head down and champed the vegetation, but Luke, though starving after all the exercise, couldn't bear the thought of eating any kind of grass, especially the scorched scrub of the paddock. Instead, he looked for a means of escape. He quickly realised the field was right next to the road so he wasted no time in jumping out and galloping off in the direction from which they had come.

Luke felt much more in control of his body now, and as light as a feather without Dino and the stolen silver on board. Nevertheless, he was exhausted from his night trek and didn't get far before he had to stop to catch his breath. He realised he had stopped next to a vegetable garden, so he broke in and happily filled his gurgling stomach on the carrots and greens.

Unfortunately, he didn't see the owner of the garden sneak up behind him. Luke was only aware of the man and his stick when it thwacked onto his rump. Luke's response to the shock and the pain was automatic, for a donkey. He threw his weight onto his front legs and let fly with his hind legs. The man was kicked to the floor and Luke tried to get away but now there was a woman charging at him with another stick. She screamed at him as she ran: 'How dare you kick my husband you wicked ass! I'll show you a beating!'

Luke turned and galloped the opposite way, back to the farm. But the thieves were out on the road looking for him so there was no avoiding being caught by someone. He was led back to the farmyard, tied up, and given another beating for running away. After the anxiety about the whole experience and the adrenaline of his escape attempt, the biting pain of the whipping easily created a disturbance in Luke's rear end and he squirted out manure all over his persecutor. Dino ran off, stinking and disgusted. In spite of his discomfort, Luke thought it was pretty hilarious and his laughter came out as a series of snorts.

Once Dino had cleaned up, the thieves returned to the yard, tacked up the donkeys, and went on their way. Luke was now totally exhausted and wished with all his heart that he had just had a lie down at the farm instead of trying to get away. The sun was out in full force and Luke's legs and back ached. It had never occurred to him how hard animals worked for humans. Thank goodness for cars, even if they did pollute, he thought.

Cico and Luke were so tired that they each stopped frequently. But even though Luke was certain that he couldn't go on, like Cico he was forced into it to escape being beaten with the stick. 'Why doesn't Dino realise how tired we are?' he thought. 'At this rate, it won't be long before I drop down dead... Hey! That's an idea! I'll just fall down, put up with Dino's beatings until they get worried about the time they're wasting, and then they'll leave me behind.'

Just as Luke finished forming his plan, he was beaten to it by old Cico who collapsed and didn't get up despite the thieves' vicious attempts at encouragement. Realising that the donkey was done-in, Dino decided that they couldn't afford to wait for him to recover, just as Luke had predicted.

But rather than leaving the donkey on the road, Dino took out a gun and shot Cico square on his forehead. Luke's four knees quivered and he felt even more faint and weak.

'That could have been me!' he thought. Apart from his trembles, he was paralysed with fear. These weren't men to play games with. He would have to do everything they asked or it could be the end for him too. If he didn't really die of exhaustion first.

Poor Cico's lifeless leggy corpse was pushed down the hillside. Luke turned away; he couldn't bear to watch. 'Poor Cico,' he thought, bidding him goodbye. 'But you saved my life, and I'll never forget you for that.' Remembering his near miss again made Luke's skin crawl and his hair stand on end despite the heat.

They set off again, Valentino on foot now. He soon moaned about his tiredness ('He thinks *he's* tired!' thought Luke) but Dino promised that they were almost there.

Just as the sun was going down, they arrived at a farm. Luke snuffled a sigh of relief, thinking this was journey's end. But the thieves didn't usually steal from houses close to them. Even in this rough terrain the police could cover more ground than them as they were equipped with quad bikes. So Luke was loaded into a lorry for the last stretch of the journey. At least he was relieved of his heavy load but his legs still had to work hard to keep him upright as the lorry careered uncaringly round the bends of the dusty track. His heart sank as the thieves took him further and further from Caravalla and humanity.

Eventually they pulled up and Luke was offloaded outside a tumble-down house, which had to be the thieves' hide-out. At last he could rest, and then think of a way to escape.

Luke was led into the house and tethered inside, having to remain hidden just like his captors. There was an old woman inside cooking. It was supposed to be supper, but it was nearer breakfast time. She took pity on Luke and gave him some water and vegetable scraps. Luke couldn't lie down as his tether was tied too short. Instead, he tried to rest a leg and doze as horses and donkeys do but he found it impossible to sleep standing up. Just as he dozed off he suddenly felt like he was falling over and he awoke with a start. Instead of sleeping, Luke rested each of his legs in turn while he stuck his nose into the robbers' business.

Dino and Valentino had just sat down at the table when the walls shook to the door-slamming entrance of a second pair of thieves carrying more stolen goods. Luke spied on what was going on through the holes in the walls of the old house. The second pair of bandits joined Dino and Valentino at the table and the old woman then walked endlessly back and forth between the kitchen and the dining room carrying plates of meat, steaming pots of tender vegetables and loaves of freshly-baked bread. The smell was making Luke ravenous and his mouth was watering as he helplessly eyed the thieves devouring their meal. The vegetable peelings had done little to quieten his growling stomach.

When the thieves were full Dino stood up and bashed his knife on the table to command silence.

'S been a few days, eh, guys? So let's 'ave a little catch up an' you can tell me why you've come back two men down. Valentino an' me 'ave had a right successful raid. We cleaned out Riccardo Valli's house in Caravalla. Ya know, the geezer that's so poor he don't have electricity but really he's loaded 'cause he's got the only successful farm there. We boshed the old man on the 'ead and cleared 'is 'ouse. An' we checked under the bed and what did we find but this little strong box, 'ere.

And it's fulla dosh, the miserly swine!'

Luke had trouble fully understanding the thieves as they had strong accents and used a lot of slang. But he got the gist of it, and jerked his head up in surprise at the news of Riccardo's money.

'We even got free rides most of the way back. So I fink we did better'n you, Gianni, 'specially since you seem to 'ave come back without Marco and Fabi,' Dino scolded.

'They may be gone,' Gianni answered, 'but I bet we've still made more money than you, like.'

Dino shrugged off Gianni's attempt to get one over on him. Losing people was risky as they might squeal to the police. Better to get less but get home.

'First we lost Fabrizio, our mastermind,' Gianni continued, making a dig at Dino who reckoned he was the brains. 'He broke into an old woman's cottage to clear her house while she was asleep, like.'

'Pah!' Dino snorted. 'Why bother? An old woman's not gonna 'ave anything worth stealing!'

"Cause it's easy pickings, like, isn't it? All we had to do was stand under the windows while Fabi threw the things out to us, there wan't no danger, like. Not 'til Fabi went to clear the old woman's bedroom anyway.'

'Some mastermind!' Dino interrupted again.

'Well, she was sleeping like a baby, he were just seizing a good opportunity, like. But she woke up and screamed "What are you doing? Throwing my tatty old things into my rich neighbour's garden?!" Fabi were taken in –'

Dino snorted contemptuously again, knowing where the story was going.

'– and he went to the window to check where he'd been throwing the stuff and whether the old woman did have a rich neighbour. Then the old woman leapt out of bed and pushed Fabi out the window. He grabbed the windowsill and hung for a bit, like, but she hit his fingers with her walking stick, and he had to let go and he broke both his legs. The old lady's screams were waking the neighbours so we had to get out of there fast. Carrying Fabi would have slowed us down so we had to leave him. He'd have done the same to any one of us.

'Then the three of us decided to find a really rich man to rob to make up for losing Fabi. In the third town we came to we were just about to go into a café for lunch when a van pulled up. We could hear something roaring inside the van so we asked the woman driving it what she had in the back. She said she was delivering a tiger to the mayor, 'cause he was so wealthy he could afford exotic pets, like. So we'd found our wealthy man. We knocked the woman out, stole the van and drove it out of town. Then we killed the tiger and skinned it and laid the skin out in the sun. We made a fire and cooked a tasty coupla tiger steaks while we waited for the skin to dry.

'Then Marco said he'd put the skin on to get into the mayor's house. Totally impossible otherwise, like, 'cause of the security. Marco would then open the front door in the middle of the night so that Emilio and I could get in and crack the safe. We stitched Marco inside the skin and put him in the cage, making sure Marco could let himself out, like.

'In the evening we wheeled Marco down the road to the mayor's house. The butler answered the door and I put on a posh voice so as not to look suspicious, like, and said "We're here to deliver the tiger." Marco roared, right on cue. The butler fetched the mayor and Marco rushed at the bars, snarling, to stop him getting too close for a good look. It was obvious the mayor was scared, like, but he pretended to be dead excited and dashed in to fetch his wallet to pay us. Then his staff took Marco inside and Emilio and me went and hid in the woods until just before midnight.

Then we went back to the mayor's house. Marco had crept out of his cage and opened the door for us. He'd seen the layout of the house, like, so he already knew where the mayor's safe would be and took us to the room. He stayed in his disguise and kept watch to frighten off anyone who came snooping. We broke the safe open and filled our sacks with the money and jewels. There was loads, man – you shoulda seen it – and Emilio and me took a load to our hiding place while Marco finished emptying out the safe for when we came back, like.

'But when we got back to the mayor's house Marco was surrounded by loads of people and they all had sticks and dogs. He tried to make a dash for it but they set their dogs on him and he couldn't out-run them. The dogs bit him and Marco yelled out which gave the game away. The dogs were called off and the people ripped the tiger-skin off to find Marco. One guy went to check the safe then and found it empty. There was nothing we could do to save Marco, like, 'cause there were too many of them so we had to make a run for it before they found out that not all of the mayor's things were in Marco's sack.'

'Well I 'ope Marco and Fabrizio keep their mouths shut about the rest of us or we'll 'ave to pay 'em a surprise visit. A nasty surprise, heh heh! All the stash you've brought back ain't wurf nofink if we're caught,' Dino said. 'An' we'd better look for some new blood too. But let's get some shut-eye 'cause we've our special raid to go on tonight.'

Dino gave the old woman stern instructions to wake them at nightfall and the thieves slid back in their chairs and fell into a drunken sleep. Luke found the thieves' snoring soothing and he too finally fell asleep.

5 ESCAPE ANTICS

Luke slept so soundly that the thieves didn't wake him when they left that evening, not even with the revving engine of the lorry which they were returning to the farm.

He did wake up when they came back though, at the sound of a girl's screams. Luke jerked his head up as the bandits brought her, screaming and squirming, into the house. She was about eighteen and the most beautiful girl Luke had ever seen. When he tore his eyes away from her face, Luke noticed her expensive clothes and guessed that she came from a wealthy family and had been kidnapped by the thieves to be held to ransom.

Dino did what he could to calm her down.

'Look, Carina, love, there's no point screaming 'cause we're in the middla nowhere 'ere an' no one'll 'ear ya. But if ya keep us awake all night you'll only make us angry and ya don't wanna do that. As long as you be'ave yourself, you're perfickly safe. We don't *want* to 'urt ya, we want to send ya back to Mummy and Daddy, which is what you want too. Ya won't be 'ere long - they'll pay up pronto.'

Carina's screams became sobs and she stopped struggling. The thieves seized their opportunity to lead her into the room that Luke was in and tied her up securely next to him. After the thieves had gone to sleep for the rest of the night, Luke nuzzled Carina's bound hands sympathetically.

'I'm sorry,' she said. 'I haven't got anything to eat, poor thing! Huh! Poor you? Poor me! It's all very well those buffoons saying I won't be here long, but they've still ruined everything. I was supposed to get married tomorrow but now I'm tired and dirty and locked up like a criminal.' She burst into tears again. As the moonlit minutes went by her wails subsided into sobs, and her sobs to purring snores when she fell asleep.

The next morning, the thieves ate a hearty breakfast while Carina was only given some bread but she was too busy crying again to eat it. Luke had a bit of luck as the thieves didn't have any animal feed and so the old lady had given him a mash of cooked wheat which, though stodgy, was more palatable than he imagined hay would be.

'You need to keep your strength up when you're working for this lot,' she whispered to him, giving him a scratch behind his ears.

With a full stomach for the first time in what seemed like ages Luke went with the thieves to retrieve the hoard stashed away from a raid prior to Carina's kidnap last night. Luke's legs were still tired from the previous journey and sleeping standing up, which made the hoard seem even further away. Dino and Gianni were taking it in turns to ride him.

'If only we coulda broken the safe of that pesky girl's 'ouse. A sackful of cash'd be much better'n 'avin' to listen to 'er screams and tears all the time. She's doin' my head in,' Dino said.

'Yeah, me too!' said Gianni. 'Perhaps gagging her would help?'

'Maybe,' Dino acknowledged.

Luke thought it odd that everyone seemed to keep all their money and valuables in their homes until he realised that banks weren't exactly handy round here. Even if the country people weren't too set in their old-fashioned ways to use phone or internet banking, the money they earned was cash in hand and you couldn't send that down a phone line.

The stash was nearly half a day's travel away. Once they had collected the loot, Luke was whipped all the way home to get him to move faster since the thieves were anxious not to be seen with the goods in broad daylight. Luke stood on a sharp stone and felt intense pain in the sensitive part of his hoof. It hurt every time he put pressure on it which slowed him down considerably.

'Get on!' Dino said, whacking him a few times.

'How long are we going to waste good food on this donkey of yours?' Gianni asked. 'He's ugly and lazy and now he's lame too. He'd be better on us dinner plates, like.'

'Yeah, all right. I'll sort it when we get back to the 'ouse.'

Luke threw his head up in fear at this and tried to move faster in the hope that if he showed willing he would change the thieves' mind.

Fortunately for Luke the loot was at the forefront of the thieves mind on their return.

'Where are Emilio and Valentino?' Gianni asked the old woman.

'They've gone to Pietro's farm for food,' she said.

'Great! We get first choice,' Dino drooled. He failed to tie Luke up securely in his hurry to fight Gianni for the best of the spoils. Luke realised that he had a chance to escape and tugged on his rope, pulling the loose knot undone. Carina saw what he was doing and said: 'Oh, you clever donkey! I only wish you could chew through my ropes.'

Luke understood her perfectly, of course, and relishing the opportunity to be a hero, he chewed at Carina's ropes on her arms and legs.

'Oh, how unusual, you've got blue eyes!' she said noticing them for the first time now her vision wasn't blurred by tears.

Once free of her bonds she jumped onto Luke's back. The old woman heard his hooves on the stone floor as Luke made his way out of the house and she came running after him to catch his trailing rope. But Luke's determination was fuelled by his desire to save his damsel in distress and so he put his heart into a turn of speed, despite the pain in his foot, and managed to out-run the aged woman.

'Oh, you're wonderful, blue-eyes!' Carina trilled. 'When we get back to my house, I'll make sure you're well rewarded. You'll have the best food and the nicest stable, and you'll never have to do a scrap of work again in your whole life.'

That sounded extremely promising to Luke right now and encouraged him to keep going in spite of his bruised foot. If he did have to stay as a donkey for the rest of his life it wouldn't be so bad if he got looked after by a gorgeous girl. And there'd be no more school!

Luke was still busy imagining his plush new lifestyle when they reached a junction in the road. Luke was about to turn left, assuming that the farm he could see in the distance on the right-hand road was where Valentino and Emilio were. But Carina said: 'What are you doing, silly? My house is this way. Oh, come on!' She kicked Luke's sides hard. Luke refused to do what she wanted, but was unable to go his own way with Carina pulling his head with the rope in the opposite direction. They stood at the junction arguing in this way until Emilio and Valentino came round the corner. Before Luke had a chance to react, the two bandits had realised what was going on. Swearing at Luke, they caught hold of his halter and Emilio gave him a thrashing.

Luke and Carina were led, struggling, back towards the run-down house. Dino, Gianni and the old woman were all still out, looking for Carina and the donkey.

Valentino asked what they were going to do with their captives now that just tying them up didn't seem to work. 'That was a close one. If she'd managed to tell anyone about us we'd be finished!'

'We'll do away with the donkey, like,' Emilio said. 'Then if she escapes again, she won't get so far. The donkey's not worth anything. He's lame, he's eating our food, and I don't like the look of him anyway; them blue eyes are freaky. I wonder what donkey burgers taste like?'

Valentino wasn't sure he wanted to know. He liked animals, and what Dino had done to that old donkey had already turned his stomach.

Valentino was a recent recruit to the gang. He'd wanted to shock his strict parents, but being a bandit had never fulfilled its promise of glamour and excitement. The reality was hiding all the time in this wreck of a house. Although they did steal a lot of valuable stuff, they had to save it for the day when they left the area and could sell it in a place where people wouldn't recognise their old belongings. The reality was a weight of constant guilt and fear. And now the reality was kidnapping girls and eating pets. It was all too uncivilised and frighteningly brutal for Valentino. He decided to wait for a quiet moment and then sneak off back to his parents with his Armani shirt tails between his legs.

If Valentino wasn't taking the serving of Luke for supper too well, Luke was in even more of a state. The chances of being able to escape a second time were almost zero. He would put up a fight, of course, but he wouldn't be able to defeat four men. Unless a miracle happened, it looked like he was doomed.

The sound of the front door slamming interrupted his thoughts. The whole house shook with the bang as Dino, Gianni and the old woman entered, bringing a stranger with them. 'Who's he?' Luke wondered. 'Another kidnap victim? But he's not tied up, and he doesn't look like he'd fetch much of a ransom.' The man was filthy and dressed in rags. There was something odd about him though. He had shaved recently for one thing. And he lacked the gleam of the desperado in his eye.

'Thank goodness you found 'em!' Dino said. 'That was a close one, eh? You wanna watch it Carina, love. You're starting to look like more trouble than you're worth and we know how to deal with trouble. One more false move and –' he sliced his finger across his throat. 'Hey, fellas, look what *we* found. This 'ere's Luciano. 'E was begging on the road, and I says to 'im: "Whatcha wanna beg for when you could steal?" so he's joining our gang.'

'All right?' Luciano inquired of the gang in a rough accent like Dino's. 'I'd be proud to join you if you'll 'ave me. I 'aven't always been a beggar; I was a leader of a gang of thieves in Lazio but I were the only one not to get caught and banged up so I came north looking for somewhere to start again.

'My clothes got all tattered and folk thought I was a beggar and started givin' me money so I thought I might as well do it for real. But begging ain't nofink like burgling 'cause ya don't make much money an' there ain't much thrill in 'aving somefink given to you instead of taking it, right? An' I didn't really need it 'cause I still 'ave a million euros which the police didn't find when they arrested my gang. I'll give it to you if you like, as a fee for joining youse?'

Through the hole in the wall, Luke saw the thieves' eyes sparkle as soon as the money was mentioned. No doubt they would have stolen it if it hadn't been offered to them. They unanimously agreed to recruit Luciano and sat him down at the table. The old woman rushed about her evening routine, doling out the food she had been cooking all day.

The bandits celebrated the arrival of their new recruit in a big way, and the poor old woman exhausted herself further carrying heavy beer crate after heavy crate until the bandits got so drunk that they passed out. Valentino, however, had only pretended to join in the festivities, and when the rest of the gang passed out he sneaked out of the door to embark on his sorry journey home.

Luke was as happy as the bandits about their new recruit. He had been forgotten about temporarily and now that they were all asleep he seized his last chance to escape. He started to gnaw at his rope again but was startled by the sound of footsteps approaching his room. His heart thumped in panic. Emilio must be awake after all and was going to kill him! Luke tugged urgently at his tether, hoping that the rickety wall itself would give way under his four-legged strength but nothing had budged by the time the door slowly opened. Luke was confronted with the ominous silhouette of a man, made twice as large by the shadows cast by the lantern in the other room. Luke felt all four of his legs quake with fear.

'Please don't kill me!' Luke brayed in terror as the

looming shadow approached. The man shushed him urgently afraid the thieves would wake up, but they were too deeply asleep to hear anything. The only person Luke wakened was Carina. Her mouth opened and vacuumed in breath in preparation for a hearty scream.

'Carina! It's me! Shh, don't make a noise,' the man hissed at her.

'Vittorio?!' Carina whispered. 'What are you doing here?'

'I've come to save you of course! I walked the roads dressed as a beggar in the hope of coming across the kidnappers. It took all day but I eventually bumped into some of them and convinced them to let me join them. They're all passed out and I've tied them up. So, come on, let's get you out of here.'

Vittorio helped Carina onto Luke's back like a true gentleman, and all three of them left the house. It was slow going as Vittorio was on foot and Luke's hoof was still sore, but there was no hurry as the bandits were safely tied up.

By dawn Luke found himself limping up the driveway of an impressive villa. The group's approach was spotted by a policeman in one of the many cars parked outside the house, and he alerted the whole household. The family and domestic staff came streaming out of the mansion to engulf Carina in hugs and tears, and sang the praises of brave Vittorio. After making sure Carina was all right, Vittorio set off with the contingent of police to guide them to the thieves' house to arrest them all.

All the belongings which the robbers had stolen were to be returned to their rightful owners. Luke was sure that the authorities would assume that he was Riccardo's donkey and he would now make it back to Caravalla. It was Sunday today, so the class was due to go home tomorrow. It wasn't likely that he'd get there and become human again in time to go with them, but at least he wouldn't be far behind.

In the meantime, Carina had insisted that the stable manager give Luke the best treatment as a reward for his part in her rescue.

Luke lapped up the luxury. He was so hungry that his mouth even watered when his warm bran mash arrived, flavoured with juicy apples. Afterwards, he lay down gratefully on his thick bed of straw. 'I won't even have to make my bed in the morning!' he thought as he drifted off to sleep.

The Micklemarshers left on Monday morning as planned, even though they had wished and prayed so hard that their return journey wouldn't be like this, that Luke had turned up and everything was all right. But it wasn't all right, and they were not all right. Some of the girls even started crying as the bus pulled out of the town square.

Chris tried to play for laughs at first to hide his own shock and cheer everyone up. 'Oh come on! He's just been turned into a frog by Serena Valli because he found out she's a witch! All he needs to do is get kissed by a girl and he'll be coming home.' No one laughed. Chris slithered down his seat and stared glumly out of the window into the growing distance like everyone else.

Jamie wondered if the joke could possibly be the truth. But if it was what could he do about it? No one would believe him if he said that. Even if he was believed they'd never be able to find a frog. He might have been squished under the wheels of a cart by now. Whatever had happened to Luke, they might never see him again.

Jamie had argued that he should stay behind to help in any way he could. But Luke's grandparents were there now and had insisted that Jamie should go home where his own mum and dad were desperate to see him safe and sound. At least with Giorgio and Bella staying at the Vallis, Jamie didn't feel like he was abandoning his friend.

Giorgio Silvester had had a blazing argument with his son on the phone. Peter was on the oil rig and said his boss wouldn't give him time off to go to Italy. Giorgio didn't think Peter was trying hard enough. It was a family emergency and Luke was Peter's son, for goodness' sake. Peter should do whatever it took to get to Italy. Even Janine was worried crazy about Luke despite saying she hated his guts every time they argued. Giorgio had made Janine stay at home with Francesca to protect her from the stress and to make sure she didn't miss any school since she was sitting her GCSEs next summer.

'But Peter should be here,' thought Giorgio. 'Bella and I aren't young anymore. We're so tired with all this worry. Peter should be here for us too. Families need to come together in times of crisis.' But Peter had said until there was some news there wasn't any point in making trouble at work, and so Giorgio and Bella would have to cope as best they could.

On Wednesday evening there was a knock on the door of Riccardo's house. Riccardo crouched behind it and timidly shouted: 'Who is it?'.

'It's Sergeant Morabelle, Signor Valli,' came the resounding reply.

'Are you sure?' Riccardo asked.

'Of course I'm sure! Open the door, Signor, I have some good news for you.'

'Luke?' Riccardo asked hopefully, warily opening the door a crack.

'Ah, no, Signor, I'm afraid not Luke.'

On seeing that it really was the sergeant, Riccardo called: 'Signor and Signora Silvestre, it's the police!' A pale-faced Giorgio and Bella came charging to the door.

'What is it, what's happened?' Bella trilled. 'Is Luke all right? Is he with you?' she asked Sergeant Morabelle urgently. Marcy emerged from her parents' room where she was sleeping while Giorgio and Bella stayed in her room.

'No, we don't have Luke, I'm afraid,' she heard the sergeant say. 'We have some news, that's all. The thieves were arrested on Monday night thanks to the brave exploits of a young man in Borenze. The police in Borenze are busy cataloguing everything at the thieves' hideout and you'll soon have back all the possessions you stated were stolen. Are you sure you didn't have any cash about the place, Signor Valli?'

'Yes. All of the little money I make is quickly spent. Why?'

'There was a substantial sum of money found at the bandits' house which no one claimed was missing. It's probably money they've made from selling stolen goods, but we're just making sure it didn't belong to anybody.'

'What'll happen to it?' Serena croaked hoarsely. She had turned a paler shade than usual.

'At the moment, it's at the police station in Borenze, but if we can't find an owner it'll eventually go to the government, I suppose. And as for Luke, Signor and Signora Silvestre, I'm afraid there was no trace of him at the thieves' dwelling, and they've denied all knowledge of the boy, even under interrogation.' He coughed here, hinting that the interrogation may have been a bit more persuasive than mere questions. 'So we can only conclude that he ran away."

'Oh, no, he'd never run away. He's a good boy!' Giorgio exclaimed.

'Well, before they left, one of the pupils...' the

Sergeant checked his notebook '...a Jamie Healey – Luke's best friend? – said Luke wasn't happy here. Maybe he tried to make his way home. Perhaps you and your wife should go home in case he does turn up there. There's nothing you can do here anyway. But we're still doing everything we can to find him, of course,' he added quickly to reassure the Silvesters who now had startled expressions on their faces. 'We'll notify you as soon as there's any news.'

Bella sighed, tears running down her cheeks. 'Oh, I suppose you're right. I just hope he's all right.'

'But didn't you find any donkeys?' Marcy asked.

'There were signs that a donkey had been tethered inside but there wasn't one there when the police raided the place. I've no idea where he is now.'

'Just one donkey?' Marcy felt close to tears. Where was Luke if he wasn't at the hide-out?

6 A TRUTH REVEALED

Luke was bored. He had nothing to do but eat and sleep, and neither of those were very pleasant any more. He tried to keep his toilet trips as far into the corner of the stable as possible, but his bed still got damp and the smell made eating even more difficult.

At first he ignored the spikes protruding from the bulging hay net, hoping to manipulate the stable manager into giving him bran mashes again instead. But the manager said 'It's no good expecting anything else. I'm not wasting good feed on a lazy donkey. If you're hungry you'll eat what you're given.'

Luke was hungry and had no choice in the end but to give up on his hunger strike and eat the hay.

He carefully stretched his neck towards the net, targeting one of the protruding stalks. But his face wasn't designed for precision anymore. His long nose got in the way of his vision, and he missed grabbing the stalk between his teeth, feeling it jab into his soft muzzle instead.

'Ow!' he said, which came out as a snort of disdain.

The snort made his nostrils vibrate, which tickled.

He tried to reach his hand up to scratch, but his arm was now a front leg and it didn't bend the right way. He didn't trust using his back leg to do the job gently enough. He had to resort to rubbing his face on the stable door to scratch it.

He fared a bit better on the second attempt, this time stabbing his gums. 'All this pain for a bit of dry grass,' he wailed to himself. 'I'd rather go out in the paddock and try eating the real grass. At least that wouldn't fight back.'

The third time he got it right, grabbing the stalk between his teeth and pulling to extract it from the net. But once it was free he couldn't manoeuvre it into his mouth. He was back to square one. This time, he chose a strand that was sticking further out of the net. He didn't close his teeth around it until he had plenty in his mouth. He used his tongue to push the hay between his molars, but a single strand was too small for his big teeth to chomp on. Luke sighed. He was going to have to go for it and grab a big mouthful.

He put his mouth to the net and used his tongue to feel around for a hole. Then he grabbed some hay, pulled it a little, grabbed more, pulled again, and so on until he had a good mouthful. He had to really tug to separate his prize from the net. The net came with him and then bounced back against the wall as he freed his mouthful. A small cloud of dust was whumped into the air. Luke coughed and sneezed and dropped his mouthful on the floor.

After he recovered he went back to the hay net. This time he got as far as chewing. The hay was spikey and dry in his mouth. It made his jaw ache to chew it and it scratched his throat when he swallowed.

He sighed sadly, his lungs wheezing with the dust. He wished more than ever to be home now. He wanted to play his games and watch TV. He wanted to mooch about with his friends. He really missed everyone, especially his family who seemed more than a few countries away now. He hadn't seen them for nearly two weeks. The worse thing was that this was all his own fault. He should never have drunk that potion. He vowed that if he ever did get out of this mess, he'd never be so reckless again.

Why hadn't the police taken him back to Caravalla? Luke couldn't believe Riccardo wasn't raising hell to get his donkey back.

Poor Luke had neither pleasant thoughts nor company to help pass his time and distract him from his gritty food. He hadn't seen Carina since their escape. She had been busy re-arranging her wedding and had since moved out of her parents' house, forgetting all about her hairy saviour.

Luke wasn't the only one to realise that Carina had forgotten about him. The stable manager had also noticed that the new donkey had been neglected and was using up valuable hay and stabling for nothing. There was an opportunity there. He would sell the donkey but carry on claiming the cost of his upkeep from his boss and make himself a double profit.

Luke was sold a few days later. He was doubly alarmed by this. It looked like no one knew that he had been stolen from Caravalla and being sold could only mean one thing: work. But surely, since he had had so much rotten luck lately, it was about time that something went right for him? Maybe Rodrigo, his new owner, wouldn't need him much.

Rodrigo was imposingly tall and thin with a sour-looking red face, and Luke took an instant dislike to him. Rodrigo's puny frame surprised Luke as he was a miller, which involved lifting heavy bags of flour. But Luke soon saw how Rodrigo avoided as much of the hard graft as he could. He had purchased Luke to carry the heavy bags of unprocessed and milled wheat, and he made his customers do most of the lifting.

Luke would have found the work strenuous at the best of times but his foot still hadn't fully healed, and after his few days of opulence he was stiff from lack of exercise. He wondered what had happened to Rodrigo's last animal. It was presumably dead of old age, or else Rodrigo had run it into the ground, which Luke thought was more likely.

Luke miserably puffed and panted his way over the hot Apennines, much to Rodrigo's disgruntlement. 'Get along, you fat lazy beast,' he cried, thwacking his stick on Luke's bony flank. 'Damn it, it's true you get what you pay for.'

After the day's work, Luke was turned out into a small, bare field with no shelter from the sun. It was the first time he had been untethered and outside since the first day of his capture, but now he didn't have the energy to escape. He sank to the ground in misery. He was too hot to nibble at the few patches of grass that, though dry, were still better than the hay. He was too exhausted to swatch at the buzzing flies with his tail. He was too tired to fall asleep and get some rest. Instead he stared dozily at the neighbouring farmer's barn.

Luke managed to prick his ears in surprise some time later when he saw Rodrigo emerge from the barn carrying a sack of wheat. Of course Rodrigo had to get his raw material from somewhere. Why not his neighbour? It probably cost less from there as the farmer wouldn't have the added transportation costs. But how come the stingy miller was doing the heavy work himself? Why hadn't Rodrigo forced Luke to do it, then he could carry several sacks at once? But maybe there was only one sack. Rodrigo must be doing a favour for his neighbour.

The days went by, full of impossibly hard work and never a day off for either of them.

There was no comfort for Luke at the day's end either as he was left in the grassless paddock. It seemed as though Rodrigo didn't have any spare stables; they were full of wheat and flour and were too good to waste on a donkey. But Luke dearly hoped that he would be human again soon. It was the end of September and the nights were getting colder. He didn't fancy spending the winter nights out in the open.

Riccardo answered the door to find Sergeant Morabelle on his doorstep. Behind the front gates was a horse harnessed to a covered cart.

'Good evening, Signor Valli,' the Sergeant greeted him. 'Just returning the items you had stolen. I've got it all because the thieves didn't have time to part with it.'

'Oh, that's wonderful!' Riccardo let out a whoop which brought the rest of his family to the door to see what was going on. 'Oh, I'm so grateful, Sergeant, thank you so much,' he gushed.

'Have you found our donkey yet?' Marcy asked.

'No, still no trace, I'm afraid. We can't find Arturo's sheep either. Though I still can't figure out why they took just one sheep. What would they want with it?'

'Perhaps they ate it. Or maybe Arturo just miscounted,' Serena said, a note of panic in her voice.

'Well, we'll keep trying to track your animal down if it's important. But I thought he was on his last legs anyway and you'd got a new donkey.' Sergeant Morabelle said.

'You're right, don't bother yourselves any more. This silver is cursed, you know; the thieves are doomed to a life of misery – in jail – for taking it, so they'll get their just desserts. Just concentrate on finding Luke,' Riccardo said.

'But Dad, Cico's one of the family!' Marcy cried.

'Yes but finding Luke is much more important right now.'

'Yes, what about Luke?' Serena asked. 'Any news?'

'No, I'm afraid not. We've put up "missing person" posters in all the towns and villages around here, but no one's reported seeing him. We're doing everything we can. Don't worry, he'll turn up soon,' the Sergeant tried to reassure them. But it had been two weeks since Luke had gone missing, and Riccardo and Serena couldn't help but think that that didn't bode well.

Marcy felt her secret boiling inside her.

Sergeant Morabelle helped Riccardo unload the cart and place the items back on the dresser while Serena slunk quietly off to her bedroom. Marcy crept up the stairs and heard her mum crying. She knocked softly on her door.

When there was no answer she said: 'Mum, can I come in?'

Serena didn't reply to that either, so Marcy took a deep, calming breath and went bravely in.

'Why are you crying?' she asked Serena.

'Luke, of course,' Serena sobbed. 'He's been gone for so long now, he must be … dead!'

Marcy had never seen her mum worry about someone before. She felt a twinge of jealousy that it was practically a stranger that was the cause of it but at least Marcy knew there were feelings under her mum's cool exterior. But her mum was always strong and dependable; Marcy didn't like to see her like this. She ought to own up to put her mum's mind at ease. How much trouble could she really be in anyway? It was mostly Luke's fault after all, not hers. He was the one that had stolen the potion and guzzled it down.

But how reassuring would the truth be? They still wouldn't know where Luke was or whether he was all right. Marcy decided that if her mum would agree to use magic to help find him, it was worth owning up.

'Don't worry too much. I'm sure he's all right,' she said. 'Can't you turn into a bird and go looking for him?'

'No, I'm sorry, I can't do that,' Serena said. 'You don't know how many times I've thought about it, or how often I've nearly done it. I'm worried sick about Luke and his poor family... But there are rumours going around the town. They're saying that Luke got proof that we were bewitching their vineyards so we turned him into a frog to stop him telling everyone. They've always been suspicious of me because I'm not from round here and now they're keeping a really close eye on us. If I'm seen doing any magic that'll be proof I've done wrong as far as they're concerned. I'll be put in jail and goodness knows how Dad'll cope without me.'

'*Have* you been bewitching everyone's vineyards?' Marcy asked, daringly.

'No! I told you, I only use magic for the good of the family.'

'But that doesn't mean that others might not suffer in some way.'

'Marcella! How can you think I would do something to harm my neighbours?'

'But didn't you turn one of Arturo's sheep into a donkey?'

'That was only one little sheep, Marcella. It could just as easily have been eaten by a fox or wandered over a precipice. It won't affect Arturo. Really, it's all right. But I promise there won't be anything else going on until Luke's back safe and sound.'

'But –'

'I'm sorry. But you must understand I can't help him that way.'

'I do.'

'And if I ever find out you've been trying to look for him yourself using magic, there'll be all hell to pay.'

Marcy didn't dare disappoint her mum and invoke her fury by confessing. And since Serena wouldn't help find Luke anyway, telling the truth would only do more harm than good.

From his vantage-point in the paddock, Luke often witnessed Rodrigo taking single sacks from his neighbour in the evenings. And neither Luke nor Rodrigo ever carried a bag of milled flour back to the farmer. Luke wondered what was going on. He found out ten days after his arrival as one evening, Rodrigo disappeared into his neighbour's barn, but instead of struggling out with a bag of wheat, he came flying out empty-handed and dived into Luke's field, turning Luke's rubber water trough upside down and hiding underneath it.

The farmer charged out of the barn in hot pursuit, shouting 'Stop, thief!' but he couldn't see anyone to chase. He stopped and looked around, shielding his eyes from the low evening sun. Luke realised that Rodrigo had been stealing the wheat from the farmer in order to make more money. Luke was beginning to detest money. That was all anyone ever seemed to be interested in and they didn't care who they hurt, man or beast, to get it.

Luke yearned to do something about Rodrigo's crimes after all the hard work and punishment he had endured at the hands of yet another crook.

Rodrigo was well hidden from the farmer. He cowered under the trough, his hand sticking out where he was clutching the rubber protectively over him.

The farmer slowly walked around the area, poking any hiding places and looking up any trees in the hope of finding his thief. As he drew near to Luke, Luke tried to indicate Rodrigo's hiding place by braying and shaking his head in the direction of the trough.

'Oh, have you knocked your trough over, you silly thing?' the farmer shouted. 'Well you'll have to wait 'til I've found that wretch.' The farmer's miscomprehension only served to frustrate Luke and he brayed even louder, kicking the trough.

'Shut it, you blue-eyed freak, or I'll send you to the knacker's yard!' Rodrigo hissed at him from under the trough. Luke was a little shaken by this, but he knew that if Rodrigo was caught and punished he wouldn't be able to send him anywhere. Luke realised he was running out of time as the farmer, having lost all hope of catching the culprit, had turned to go in. There was only one option left to Luke. He walked right up to the trough and stamped hard on Rodrigo's protruding hand, screwing his hoof about to maximise the pain.

'Arghhhhhhhhhhh!' Rodrigo screamed.

'Yes, you don't like pain when the shoe's on the other hoof, do you?' Luke thought.

The farmer turned around. Luke brayed in confirmation and the farmer hurdled the fence into the paddock and threw off the water trough to find his neighbour nursing a bruised and broken hand.

'You!' the farmer cried in disgust at being deceived by his own neighbour. 'I don't believe it! Well, you'll pay for this, mark my words!'

The farmer, whose hard labour had made him twice as strong as the weedy Rodrigo, dragged him up off the floor and carted him inside his house. After some time, a pair of policemen arrived and arrested Rodrigo and took him away in their dusty car.

7 SUNDAY LUNCH

Rodrigo didn't return so Luke could only assume that he had been put in jail. Luke thought urgently of escape but his unforgiving work had stopped his foot from healing so he thought it better to fully recover before making a break for freedom. With Rodrigo in jail he had plenty of time after all, especially as the kind farmer was feeding him.

With time on his hands, Luke thought a lot about Rodrigo and the bandits. Why had they been so rough on him and Cico? Wasn't it obvious that any animal would work better if it was treated kindly? If they'd travelled the road hitting another person like that they'd have caused an outrage. Why should an animal be any different?

But it wasn't just bad people who were so cruel, Luke realised. Only a few weeks ago he had hit a mouse with a magazine. Granted, he felt guilty afterwards, but he shouldn't have done it in the first place. He vowed never to be cruel to animals again and to make sure none of his friends were either. In return, he hoped that he wouldn't have to endure any more suffering on his way back to Caravalla.

'Poor thing,' the farmer said to Luke one day as he pulled his ears in a friendly gesture. 'I hear they're selling you with a load of Rodrigo's other stuff 'cause he can't afford to pay me back for the wheat he stole. Spent all his profits on drink, the fool. I hope you get a much nicer new owner; you deserve it after helping me out. I'd take you on myself but I can't afford to keep an animal I don't need.'

Luke blanched at this beneath his hide and he tested his foot but it was still sore. He knew that to escape now would make it worse again which meant he wouldn't get very far, so he decided to chance waiting for a couple of days more.

Of course by then it was too late. Bailiffs came and held an auction, selling Rodrigo's things at knockdown prices. Luke's stomach turned with anxiety at this. It was a guarantee of being sold to a poor household where he would undoubtedly be treated in a worse manner than he had so far.

Luke's assumptions were half right. On the first day of October, exactly one month after he had left his beloved home in Micklemarsh, he arrived at the home of his new owner, Mario. Mario was poor and thin and lived in a wooden shack on the small patch of land where he grew vegetables. He used Luke to carry his excess produce to market to sell.

Despite his poverty, Mario treated Luke with respect and kindness, always petting and praising him. Luke was even given a name for the first time, which pleased him, even though it was unoriginal; 'Blue' because of his blue eyes.

Mario spared what little he could to feed his indispensable companion and Luke found that his hunger was diminished by his new owner's friendship. His foot was finally better after his rest at Rodrigo's and a healing herbal poultice applied by Mario, and he worked as hard and obediently as he could. He put all thoughts of escape to the back of his mind as he couldn't possibly leave his poor friend in the lurch. Mario had spent his last cents on Luke and relied on him to make his living. Luke would just have to trust that a solution would present itself as it had in every other situation he'd been in as a donkey. He was surely due a lucky break, even if all of this was his fault.

Mario's generosity didn't stop at his essential companion. Just over a week after Luke had arrived the first autumn storm struck, and after darkness fell, there was a knock at the rickety shed door. Mario opened it to reveal a bedraggled man.

'Hi,' the stranger said. 'I was wondering if you could help me. I've just got caught out in this dreadful storm and I was wondering if I could shelter here until it stops. I always catch terrible chills if I get soaked in the rain.'

'Of course,' Mario said.

The man introduced himself as Cristiano. They tethered his fine-looking horse next to Luke in the shelter at the side of the house. It was undoubtedly not the luxury the horse was used to. After Rodrigo's barren paddock Luke was grateful he now had a roof to keep off the rain.

Mario made Cristiano a warm drink and a snack. It grew late and the storm still didn't let up, so Mario offered the man his bed for the night while he slept on the floor.

In the morning, Cristiano couldn't express his gratitude enough. He felt refreshed by his night's sleep and had undoubtedly been spared a nasty cold by Mario's kindness.

'How can I ever repay you?' Cristiano asked.

'Don't worry about it. I didn't help you so I could profit from it,' Mario assured him.

'But, still, the goodness of a heart like yours shouldn't go without its reward. At least come with me up to my farm and have Sunday lunch with me.'

Mario consented to the meal and he and Cristiano mounted their animals and travelled the few miles to Cristiano's house. Since there were no empty stalls Luke was tethered in the shady yard near the kitchen door and given hay and water.

Luke gratefully sucked in the water; he was sweltering as the previous evening's storm hadn't relieved the humid atmosphere of the Indian summer.

With the weather being so hot the kitchen door was open and a bored Luke took time out from massacring his hay net to peer in. The first thing he spied was a low-hanging joint of meat. 'That must be what they're having for lunch,' Luke thought. 'Typical! I'll have to stand here and smell all that lovely food cooking and not be able to have any of it myself! I wish I could get back to the Vallis' house and be turned back into a human. I can't wait to eat real food again. Even their food. Just a slice of bread! Mmm, freshly-baked bread...'

Luke's salivations and ruminations were interrupted by a noise behind him. He crooked his head around and saw a black Labrador prowling towards the kitchen door.

Luke realised he was after the hanging meat and tried to warn him off with a couple of kicks, but the dog dodged between his legs and got into the kitchen. The joint was hung so low that it was no problem for the large dog to balance on his hind legs, secure the meat between his teeth and paws and tear it from the hook. Luke brayed to alert the cook who was in the far corner chopping the vegetables. The dog hurriedly dragged the meat out of the kitchen, throwing Luke a burning look from his chocolate brown eyes. The chef took no notice of Luke's single bray, so Luke emitted several more to get his attention.

'Shut it, donkey!' the cook shouted, without looking up from his dextrous slicing. When Luke didn't shut up, the cook said 'What are you making that racket for?' and finally turned around. He eventually realised what was missing and cried 'Oh, I don't believe it! Damn it! How stupid can you get? I knew I should have taken the time to hang that venison properly.'

'What's going on, Orlando?' cried Luisa, the cook's wife. She worked as Cristiano's housekeeper, and had come bustling in to the kitchen to see what the catastrophe was.

'A dog's snatched the joint because I didn't hang it properly.'

'Oh, for goodness sake, Orlando. You're getting so careless. That's your third mistake this month.'

'I know. But Cristiano's such a nice man. You don't think he'll be too cross, do you?'

'Have you lost your mind as well as your meat?' Luisa shrieked. 'You can't own up to this one and he'll probably give you the sack! No, no, no! There must be a better way,' she said, her sharp eyes darting around the kitchen. 'Aha! Yep, there's a solution right under your nose.'

'If you're going to say get a replacement, I can't,' Orlando said. 'It's not like there's a herd of deer running around the back yard.'

'No, not exactly,' Luisa agreed. 'But there is a donkey.'

'But donkey meat won't taste anything like venison and it'll be far too tough.'

'It'll be fine as long as you prepare it in the right way. All you need to do is cook it slowly in plenty of water so it goes tender and make sure you use lots of herbs and spices to cover up the flavour.'

'You're right; I probably could pull that off! Luisa, baby, you're a genius!' cried Orlando and went to sharpen his knives. Luke's heart was already pounding but at that dreadful grating noise his legs shook and he felt sick. He wondered, briefly, if donkeys could actually be sick.

'Hang on, though!' Orlando was having second thoughts. 'Killing the donkey will solve the problem of the missing venison, but it'll create a whole new problem of a missing donkey. How will we cover that one up, eh?'

Luke snorted a sigh of relief.

'We'll leave a snapped piece of his halter tied to the ring and open the gate and say he ran away and we couldn't catch him.'

'Ha! Good one. Right, let's go.'

Orlando untied Luke, intending to lead him away to a secluded area for the slaughter. Luke quickly put his shaking legs to use, digging them in and pulling his head up sharply. The lead-rope began to slide through Orlando's hands causing rope burns which made him gasp and let go in pain. Luke was free but a high gate and walls enclosed the yard and the gap in the corner that the dog had used was nowhere near big enough for Luke. There was only one escape: through the house.

Luke wove his way through the challengingly man-sized spaces between the kitchen work surfaces which threatened him with pans of boiling water and sharp knives. He jumped up the few steps that led into the main part of the house and charged through the hallway, his hooves clattering on the wooden floor - the wooden floor that Luisa had just been polishing. Luke skidded past the stag heads and antique oil paintings and straight into the sitting room where Cristiano and Mario were talking animatedly about organic farming over a glass of fine wine.

'What the...?' Cristiano cried, jumping out of his chair in surprise.

'Blue!' Mario shouted. 'What are you doing in here?'

Cristiano called for his staff but Luisa and Orlando didn't come, reluctant to take responsibility and get into trouble.

'Oh, let's just go and find them. We'll leave Blue in here for now,' Cristiano said.

Luke was locked in and Cristiano marched with Mario into the kitchen to see if Orlando or Luisa knew what was going on.

'There's a rabid dog about!' Luisa invented. 'It had a go at the donkey and when the donkey broke loose it followed him into the kitchen and started attacking everything in sight. We heard you calling us but we were too busy getting rid of it to answer.'

'My goodness! Is it dead?'

'Well, I hit it a few times with my brush, but it's run off into the fields.'

'You'd better let the neighbours know to be careful. Neither of you were hurt were you?'

'What? Er, no, no, I'm okay. We're okay,' Orlando stammered.

'Well at least that's something,' said Cristiano. 'But Mario, if Blue's been bitten we'll have to put him down before he hurts anyone.' Mario nodded miserably. 'He's safe where he is just now. We'll see how he is after dinner.'

'Oh, about dinner, sir,' Orlando said.

Luisa gave him a dagger-sharp stare to stop him owning up. 'Yes,' she said. 'The dog jumped at it and sank its foamy teeth in, so we've thrown it out to be on the safe side.'

'Oh, right. Well that *is* unfortunate. I really wanted

to give my guest here a slap-up meal.'

'One of them things,' Luisa shrugged.

Luke slept soundly on the sitting room rug while Cristiano and Mario ate a distinctly meatless meal in the dining room. He awoke when he heard voices outside the sitting room door and tuned in to what was being said.

'Phew! He's very quiet,' came Mario's voice. 'He must be all right.'

'Well, it is fatal.'

'Oh, you don't think he's dead, do you? I need him!' wailed Mario. 'No, he can't be,' he decided, reason overcoming his panic. 'Not so quickly.'

'Why don't you go in and see?' Cristiano suggested.

'Uh-uh. You go in,' Mario insisted.

'He's your donkey!'

'It's your house!'

'Why don't you just open the door a crack and take a peek? No offence, but I really don't want to be injured by a rabid donkey that isn't even mine.'

After some procrastination, Mario opened the door. Luke, alerted by their exchange, realised he was at risk yet again and made sure he appeared the least deranged-looking as possible.

'He looks calm enough,' Mario told Cristiano. 'And I can't see any bite marks.'

'Let's give him a bucket of water. If he's not afraid of it, we'll know for sure that he's all right.'

The bucket of water was duly fetched and placed in the room with Luke. Mario and Cristiano then quickly retreated and watched through the gap in the door. Luke guzzled down the water without a moment's hesitation. It wasn't hard as he was thirsty anyway. The two men then approached Luke and petted him and laughed until they cried over how afraid they had been of a perfectly harmless donkey. Luke sensed, from their camaraderie, that Mario and Cristiano had become good friends.

'Well, I'd better get him home,' Mario said resignedly.

'No, listen,' said Cristiano. 'I've been on my own for some time since my divorce and my son moved to a farm of his own. I could really do with an extra pair of hands around here and I'd be honoured if you'd work for me. And there are plenty of spare rooms in this house for you to choose one to stay in.'

'Wow! Really?' Mario asked, his eyes sparkling. 'I've never had such good luck before. I'd be a fool not to say yes.'

It was a lucky break for Luke too. He never returned to Mario's old hut as Cristiano sent a van that afternoon to fetch the few belongings that Mario wanted to keep. Luke knew Cristiano wouldn't need him as his wealth and accessible land meant he had plenty of vehicles to do the work. It meant that, at long last, Luke was able to escape and try to find his way back to Caravalla.

That evening he bid a silent goodbye to Mario, glad that things had worked out so well for him. He really deserved it. Luke sailed over the low fences separating his paddock from the road. He wasn't sure of the quickest route back, but he remembered the way he had come and began to retrace his steps back towards Caravalla and humanity.

`

8 STEALING THE SHOW

Luke travelled under cover of darkness and found somewhere secluded to hide during the day when he grazed and slept. He knew someone would interfere if they came across a donkey journeying by itself.

When dawn broke on Thursday, Luke realised that the road was passing right over the hill tops and there were no woods to hide in. Luke had to settle for squatting uncomfortably in a ditch and falling into a fitful sleep.

He wasn't sure how long he had been asleep, but it didn't feel like long enough when he was woken by something sharp prodding his flanks. He raised his weary head and saw a very unkempt man prodding him with a walking stick.

'So, yer not dead,' the man said to him. 'Come on, get up then. Let's be havin' yer.'

Luke was puzzled as to what this man wanted with him and he didn't see why he should get up for him. He was his own donkey now!

But the man had other ideas. He undid his belt – made from a length of ragged rope – and tied it in a halter around Luke's head. Then he jerked and tugged at Luke while beating him with his stick. 'I said, get up!'

Luke had no choice but to stand up.

'That's better. Whatcha doin' in that ditch, eh? Homeless are yer? Then we're two of a kind. I know where you can go, an' I'll be doin' us *both* a favour.'

'What could he mean?' thought Luke as he plodded beside the man. 'Are we going somewhere for food?' Even if that was the case, Luke didn't want to go with the man. But as had so often been the case in his time as a donkey, he was powerless against a man with a halter and a stick.

The vagrant took Luke to the local market to sell him. He knew the donkey must have already belonged to someone and that he really should have reported the stray animal to the authorities. But there would have been no profit for him in that, and he had to eat.

Luke was furious at being prevented from getting back to Caravalla, either via the police or under his own steam. He was terrified that his new owners might keep him somewhere impossible to escape from and that he would be subjected to more hard labour.

As his buyers led him from the market place, he was shocked to see his human form staring at him from a sun-faded 'missing person' poster. It felt strange seeing his old self. It seemed like such a long time ago now. As he clopped past the poster, he glimpsed the moving message from his family:

"Luke, we love you. Please come home."

'If only I could,' he thought and a tear dropped from his eye.

The buyers were a sister and brother; twins called Gemma and Giorgio. It was a spur of the moment purchase as they had bought too much at the market to carry home and Luke had been so cheap.

Luke felt a pang of homesickness at the name shared with his grandfather and the trivial brother-sister arguments Gemma and Giorgio conducted on their way home.

One of the biggest disputes was what to name Luke. Gemma wanted to call him 'Blue' but Giorgio thought it wasn't inventive enough. But every time Gemma said Blue, Luke seemed to nod his head in response so Gemma declared that the donkey had decided it.

Luke liked the name. It sounded a bit like his real name, and it reminded him of Carina and Mario and made him hopeful that the twins would be just as kind to him.

When they reached their destination Luke was put in a walled yard at the back of the kitchen, similar to Cristiano's house. His heart sank at the sight of it, knowing he would never be able to jump out, and the high gates were kept padlocked. He sullenly munched the hay laid out for him and eavesdropped on the activities of Gemma and Giorgio.

It turned out that the house wasn't theirs, but their master's. They worked as chefs, preparing lavish food for the master's frequent dinner parties. Luke's involvement was to carry excess cooked goods to the market to sell, and bring home the fresh purchases. It was simple work, which didn't eat up much of Luke's day, so he spent the rest of it turned out in the courtyard.

He would stand close to the kitchen window or the open half-door, and whenever there was no one looking he picked at any remnants of food within his reach. He only took a nibble from each plate, careful to avoid getting the petty thefts noticed by his masters. Still, even if they did realise what was going on, they would never suspect the donkey of stealing the food.

But it is easier to abstain completely than to restrict yourself to only a little of something so delicious. It wasn't long before Luke was unable to resist polishing off a whole plate of fluffy roast potatoes. He licked the plate clean and then noisily sucked up the contents of the gravy boat to wash the potatoes down.

This dramatic loss of food didn't go unnoticed by the twins. Of course, it didn't occur to either of them that it could be Blue. Instead, they secretly suspected each other. After the roast potato incident Gemma and Giorgio each took an initial count of the number of leftovers. They then re-checked the goods whenever the other one wasn't around to prove their suspicions. Luke tried to break his habit at this point, knowing that were he to continue he might be found out.

It was an apple pie that got the better of Luke in the end. There was over half of it left and it was placed, still gently steaming, on the windowsill next to a jug of the creamiest custard he had ever seen. He guzzled down the lot and then wandered away from the window and pretended to busy himself in his hay manger.

Gemma entered the kitchen, dumped a tray of remainders, and passed Giorgio on her way out. Giorgio dumped his pile of washing up in the sink and instantly saw the empty plate on the windowsill above. He waited for Gemma's return with his hands on his hips, impatiently tapping his right foot.

'I don't believe you!' Giorgio shouted at his sister. 'My own twin, ripping me off by eating the leftovers so we can't sell them at market.'

'What? I certainly have not!' the innocent Gemma protested.

'Don't lie! There's been food missing for weeks!'

'I know! But you took it, not me! The cheek of it, stealing the stuff and then accusing me! And I've been turning a blind eye all this time to avoid having an argument with you.'

'Hey, I didn't do it, don't try and point the finger at me!'

'Well I didn't do it, so it must be you.'

'Why would I do a thing like that to my own sister?'

'So who *has* been stealing from us then?'

After a contemplative silence, Giorgio reasoned 'Well it's only gone missing from the areas near the window and the doors. And the only one who has outside access to them is Blue.'

'Oh, don't be silly! Donkeys don't like human food. Besides, whoever's been doing this is very cunning and a donkey is far too stupid to pull the wool over our eyes. It'll be some tramp hiding in the yard and waiting until we're out of sight before taking his fill.'

Luke was relieved that the blame had shifted from him and he made sure he kept out of sight in order not to remind the twins of the possibility that it might be him. But Luke had also put himself out of earshot and didn't hear the plan that the twins formulated in order to catch the culprit.

The next day, Giorgio and Gemma made sure to leave plenty of delicious foods near the door and window and then left the kitchen through the hallway door. They left the door open a crack and pressed their eyes to it, making sure they had a good view of the back door and window. And what should they see but Blue nosing over to the window and wolfing down some mashed potato and gnawing his way around a chicken leg?

Their indignation left them immediately and they fell through the door in hoots of laughter at the sight. The more they laughed, the more Luke realised he wasn't going to get into trouble, and the more greedily he ate.

Giorgio and Gemma laughed so long and loud that

their master came in to see what was so funny. Luke was surprised to see the TV star Enrico. He was doubly surprised to see that he, Luke, a thirteen-year-old former human being could make a clown laugh as Enrico was bent double in hysterics at the sight.

All three people had tears of mirth streaming down their faces. They clutched their stomachs in pain, gasped for breath, and laughed some more.

'This is brilliant!' Enrico finally gasped. 'On Saturday… Saturday, he must join in the dinner party and perform for my guests. They'll laugh… hahaha… they'll laugh 'til they die. Hehehe.'

So Luke was led into the dining room on Saturday evening. He had been deprived of human food since the discovery to make sure he'd have a big appetite for the performance. He was parked at the head of the table where a large space had been left for him and an oversized napkin was tied around his neck. Gemma and Giorgio served food onto the plate in front of him. Luke was served each delicacy individually as the guests longed to discover how fussy an eater the donkey would be.

The first dish was spaghetti Bolognese. Luke chomped at the meatballs with his teeth and then sucked up the strands of spaghetti as humans do. Then he licked the dripping sauce from his lips. The guests laughed.

'I'm sure that if he could, he would dab his mouth with the napkin!' Enrico called. 'Now what about these? Surely he won't like pickled onions?'

Luke wolfed them down, snorting slightly at their acidity.

'Well, he won't like this chicken curry, it'll be too spicy.'

Luke knew he would, it was his favourite. He nosed round the herby pieces of meat first, picking them up and chewing them, then he moulded his lips to the necessary shape and sucked the creamy sauce up. Then he licked the plate clean.

A cheer of 'Bravo!' reverberated around the table.

Luke hung his tingling tongue out of his mouth.

'Oh, get the poor thing some water!' someone hollered.

'No, no, not water, try some lager!'

Luke licked his lips in anticipation and everyone laughed. Gemma had trouble pouring the lager into a jug because she was shaking with laughter. When it was offered to him, Luke picked the large vessel up with his teeth, tipped his head back and slurped noisily at the contents. The metallic taste and fizziness of the lager made him contort his face into shapes which the guests found hilarious. Then, of course, Luke let rip.

'Ee-waaaaarrrrr.'

The guests laughed until they slithered onto the floor. Even Luke, a little giddy from the lager, found his own behaviour absurd and tried to laugh too: 'He-har, he-har, he-har.' He finished with a 'Hic-a' as he developed hiccups and the guests kicked their feet and slapped their hands on the floor. Since everyone was fully occupied with their convulsions of laughter and no longer paying Luke any attention, he made a start on the pudding, if only to remedy his hiccups. When the hysterics finally died down, Enrico managed to say:

'Gemma and Giorgio, you'll have to get yourself a new donkey. Blue is far too clever for just going to market. I'm going to train him up to appear on my show.'

Luke was massively excited about the prospect of being a TV star, even if it was in the guise of a donkey. Enrico was as kind to Luke as Gemma and Giorgio had been but the work was even easier than his daily trip to market. All Luke had to do was behave as much like a human as possible, and he had had plenty of experience of that.

By the end of the next day the pair had devised a sketch for broadcast. For the first time since having four legs, Luke got to travel in style. On Monday he was loaded into a luxurious horse box and driven to the TV studios in Florence. The studio crew built the required set and Luke rehearsed to perfection in time for Tuesday night's live recording.

'And now, for the first time on television, please welcome the latest addition to my bizarre circus... Signor Donkey!'

The audience clapped in half-hearted acknowledgement of the unknown performer. The television displayed an extreme close-up of something cream with a blue abstract pattern, over which a caption was super-imposed: "Doing the donkey work". The camera zoomed out and revealed the cream blur to be a duvet. Going further out, a bedroom set was revealed, and asleep in the bed was ... a donkey. The audience tittered.

A giant alarm clock went off, the donkey rolled over, shut off the alarm with his hoof and went back to sleep. A second sounding of the alarm drowned out the audience's laughter. The donkey groaned, got out of bed and the camera followed his stagger to the mirror. Signor Donkey stared haggardly at himself in the mirror and then shook himself all over. He stretched his head round and groomed his withers and checked himself again in the mirror, contorting his huge rubbery mouth into a toothy grin.

The camera pulled back to watch Signor Donkey walk down some stairs. The audience hooted with laughter. When Signor Donkey reached the kitchen he sat down on his behind and ate his continental breakfast. To the immense amusement of the audience Luke ate buttered rolls, ham, a peeled boiled egg and some orange juice. A pastry and a cup of coffee followed this. The audience was shrieking by now. Then Signor Donkey got up, picked up a briefcase in his teeth, winked into a camera close-up, and left for work.

Up came a freeze-frame of the winking donkey with the briefcase in his mouth and the caption "The End". The audience cheered and cheered and poor Enrico, petting his celebrity donkey, couldn't be heard for some time. 'There'll be more adventures with Signor Donkey on Thursday!' he shouted above the clamour.

9 RESCUE PLAN

The whole class was buzzing. Everyone was chatting excitedly about something though Marcy didn't know what. She had been late for school and didn't get in until the end of registration.

'What's everyone talking about?' she asked Nadia Moscari.

'Last night! Didn't you see it?'

'Settle down, everyone,' the teacher interrupted. 'It's time to start the lesson. I won't have any more of this noise, class.'

'See what?' Marcy couldn't bear to give up the subject just yet.

'Marcella Valli, you are about to get yourself a detention.'

'See what?' Marcy scrawled on a piece of paper.

'"Ecco Enrico!"' Nadia wrote back.

'No TV, remember? What happened?' Marcy replied, aware that "Ecco Enrico!" was the phenomenal entertainment programme everyone seemed hooked on.

'Tell you later,' Nadia responded cautiously, having witnessed the teacher's glaring eye when Marcy had passed her latest note.

Marcy fizzed with frustration until the break-time bell finally rang.

'Right,' Marcy said, 'tell me what happened on "Ecco Enrico!" last night.'

'Oh, it was so funny!' Nadia said, giggling at the memory. You must be the only person in the whole of Italy not to have seen it.'

'Yeah, yeah,' Marcy said. 'Just tell me what was so funny.'

'They had this donkey on who was pretending that he was a human who had to go to work. He was brilliant: he could lie in a bed and walk down stairs and drink coffee... it was so funny!'

'Is he going to be on again?' Marcy asked, her brain working overtime and her heart pounding.

'Enrico said he'd be back on tomorrow's show and I can't see why he wouldn't be. Everyone loved him.'

'Can I come round and watch it?'

'Yeah, sure. Come for tea, if you like.'

'And now it's time for... Signor Donkey!'

The audience clapped and cheered and stamped their feet. The screen went black and the caption "You can't teach an old donkey new tricks" came up. The camera pulled away to reveal a blackboard with multiplication sums on it. As the camera pulled further away, a stern-looking teacher was exposed, pointing a stick at one of the sums on the black board.

'Class,' said the teacher. 'Who can tell me what the square root of six hundred and twenty five is?'

There was an 'Ee-orr' and the audience laughed. The camera panned across the classroom full of boys and girls in smart uniforms and at the back of the class, sitting on the floor, was Signor Donkey. He too was dressed in a smart, though large, uniform. He was wearing giant fake glasses and was nodding his head intelligently at the teacher.

'Signor Donkey?' the teacher asked.

Signor Donkey rapped out with his hoof: 'tap tap (pause) tap tap tap tap tap'.

'Yes, that's right. It's twenty five.'

The camera cut to a shot of Enrico looking amazed and tapping the numbers into a calculator. The Donkey was correct and Enrico duly showed his proof to the camera, nodding his head and smiling.

The camera cut back to the classroom.

'Now then, class,' the teacher said, 'On the board is a simultaneous equation which I would like you to work out in your notebooks at your desks, and the first one to do it must come and write what 'x' is on the board.'

The puzzled children all scribbled busily into the books on their desk, scratching their heads. Signor Donkey waltzed straight up to the board. His mouth grabbed some chalk out of the teacher's hand and he winked a blue eye at the camera. Then, holding the chalk delicately between his teeth, next to "x =" on the board he wrote the number 2.

'That's correct!' exclaimed the teacher. 'Signor Donkey, you're top of the class!'

The shot cut to a freeze-frame of Signor Donkey, chalk in mouth, winking at the camera and "The End" was displayed.

The audience went wild and Enrico shouted above the noise 'Signor Donkey will be back next week!'

The donkey's winking blue eyes confirmed to Marcy that it was Luke. She was about to run home and tell her dad and Sergeant Morabelle that she had found their donkey, but she saw the flaw in that immediately. Their donkey hadn't had blue eyes and even if her dad could be persuaded to lay claim to Signor Donkey, Enrico would offer a lot of money to keep him, which Riccardo would accept. She would have to keep the discovery a secret and rescue Luke herself.

'Where do they record this show?' she asked the Moscaris.

'In Florence, I think,' Nadia's sister, Elena, said, typing into her phone. 'Why?'

'I have to go there.'

'Hey, yeah, what a great idea. We could go and watch it being recorded. It must be so much funnier live. Can we go, please?' Nadia asked her mum and dad.

'I don't know. How much does it cost? We've got to be careful just now, with the vines doing so badly,' Signor Moscari said.

'Yes, it's Florence. And it's free,' Elena announced from the results on her phone.

'Well, if that's the case then I don't see why not. I suppose it would do us good to get away from it all,' he said, referring to the fact that the town was still in mourning for the loss of Luke.

Now all Marcy had to do was tackle her dad for permission to go with the Moscaris.

Marcy rushed home and checked Riccardo was in a good mood before asking: 'Dad, can I go to Florence with the Moscaris on Tuesday?'

'What do you want to go to Florence for? You've been before; it's just full of old things. There's nothing new.'

'We just all thought it would be nice to have a break from Caravalla for a bit.'

'Well why don't you have a picnic in the next village then?'

'Because the next village doesn't have "Ecco Enrico!"'

'And what is "Ecco Enrico!"?'

'It's a TV show,' Marcy said reluctantly through gritted teeth.

'Nope.'

'No? No what?'

'No you can't go.'

'Why not?'

'Because the next thing I know you'll be badgering me for a TV. "Oh, Dad, it's so good. It's fun and educational and everything." Well I can't afford one, or the electricity to run it, so you can't go to Florence getting expensive ideas in your head.'

'I won't ask you for a TV, I promise. If I was that desperate to watch TV I'm sure my friends wouldn't mind if I watched it at their house. But "Ecco Enrico!" is a clown show, and they've got this particular act at the moment that's so funny. We just want to have some fun, that's all.'

'Oh, do you? Got fed up of the gloomy atmosphere because Luke's still missing, is that it? How can you think of having fun when something as terrible as that is hanging over our heads?'

'Because Luke's disappearance is the only thing I've been thinking about for the past two months. It's not that I don't feel bad, it's just that I need a break. Anyway if Luke did run away, Florence would be a sensible place for him to go seeing as it's the nearest big city. I might even bump into him there if I go. Who knows?'

Riccardo was swayed by the unlikely reason in the desperate hope that it would somehow come true. 'Well… how much is it going to cost?' he asked grudgingly.

'The show's free but it would be great if you have anything for me to put towards the petrol.'

'Yes, all right. It's been a while since you last had some pocket money. Go get it off your mum.'

Marcy slept right through the night for the first time in ages. She felt relieved that she was finally close to rescuing Luke and making him human again. But when she awoke, her mind refreshed, she realised her plan was still a long way from fruition. It was only Friday and she had to wait until Tuesday evening until she would be anywhere near Luke.

And there was still the problem of how she would actually get to Luke. 'There's bound to be a lot of security around a celebrity donkey, ' she thought. 'And if I do get round the security guards it'll be impossible to rescue Luke as a donkey because I'll never get him out of the building unnoticed. I'll have to take an antidote with me and get it to him somehow. Then I'll have to delay the Moscaris drive back here while Luke finds somewhere private to drink the potion and transform. And I need to give him instructions for where to meet us.'

She realised she ought to take him some clothes too as she grinned at the mental image of Luke sneaking around a film studio holding some hay over his privates. But Luke would only get that far if Marcy made the antidote correctly in the first place. She would probably only have one shot at this.

Luckily she shouldn't have a problem getting sole access to the roof since her mum had stopped practising magic. And the benefit of Tuesday being so far away was that it gave Marcy plenty of time to gain access to her mum's supplies.

Whilst her mum was out shopping on Saturday Marcy sneaked into her parents' bedroom with a torch. Thanks to her previous detective work, Marcy knew exactly where her mum kept her magic things. Marcy gripped the torch in her teeth and wriggled under the high, old-fashioned bed until she found a loose floorboard.

Under the floorboard she found Serena's bag. She fished the spell book out and found the "Antidote for Metamorphosis", copying it down so that she wouldn't have to take the book away and risk her mum noticing its absence. She rummaged for the Essence of Pupae and put a teaspoon full of it in a plastic bag before carefully putting everything back in its place. She squeezed herself out from under the bed and returned to her own bedroom.

There she hid everything along with the hairs she had saved from Luke's pillow before her mum had given up hope of his return and washed and put away his bedding.

On Monday night she waited until her parents were asleep in bed and then crept up onto the roof to cast the spell. It would be too difficult to get a liquid to Luke, but she had a clever trick in mind. She just hoped it all went to plan.

10 AT THE STUDIO

The next day, Marcy went straight to Nadia's house with her after school.

'Are you all ready?' she asked the family.

'Yes, we're just waiting on Signor Moscari,' her mum answered, her head nodding in the direction of the toilet. 'I suppose we might as well be getting in the car.'

Marcy hoped Signor Moscari wouldn't be too long. It was already after four. It would take about an hour to get to the studio on the outskirts of the city, and maybe an extra half an hour to get parked somewhere and walk to the entrance, which took them to half five as it was. There would probably already be a queue forming by then.

Nadia and Elena squabbled over not going in the middle.

'I'll go in the middle,' Marcy offered.

'No, you can't. It's rubbish in the middle and you're the guest. Elena can sit there 'cause she's the youngest.'

'No! I don't want to sit there. I'll get car sick in the middle,' Elena whined.

'I don't mind sitting there, honestly,' Marcy said.

'Just being able to go somewhere in a car is a novelty for me, so I don't mind where I sit. Just please don't fight about it anymore.'

The sisters' arguing was getting on her already overwrought nerves. They got into the car and Signor Moscari finally came out of the house and locked its sturdy wooden door.

'Okay! Everybody ready?' he said exuberantly as he thumped into the car. The car creaked ominously under his weight.

'Yes!' Everybody chorused.

'Right! Let's go!'

He put the key in the ignition and turned it. The car went 'Whir-hir' and cut out.

'Come on now,' Signor Moscari coaxed.

'Whir-hir-hir?' the car tried.

Marcy felt sick. This was not looking good. If they didn't get there on time, they wouldn't get in. And even if she managed to stay behind to gain access to Luke later, she only had until half past eleven before the twenty-four hour potion lost its efficacy. The whir-hir process was repeated several times until Signor Moscari gave up.

'I'm sorry, kids. It's just not been used for so long.'

'You have got petrol in it, haven't you?' Signora Moscari nagged him.

'Yes, look the gauge says it's full. The car's just out of practice that's all. It's forgotten how to work. I'll look under the bonnet.'

'Well don't get your good clothes dirty!'

'Aww, mum! We really want to go!' Elena whined after her dad exited the vehicle.

'I know, dear. Are you all right, Marcella?' she asked, suddenly noticing Marcy's pallid face.

'I'm fine.'

'Are you sure? You don't look well.'

'I'm just worried we're not going to be able to go, that's all.'

'Well, we're not beaten yet, so keep your spirits up. We can always go another day, anyway.'

That didn't cheer Marcy up much. Now she had a chance, she just wanted to get this mess tidied up. And she only had a limited supply of hair from Luke's pillow.

'I can't see anything wrong with the engine,' Signor Moscari broke Marcy's chain of thought with the sudden appearance of his face through the window. 'Maybe we should try giving it a push start.'

It was fortunate that they were in the Apennines, as there were plenty of hills for the four females to push the car down. Signor Moscari sat in the driving seat whir-hirring the engine. Marcy desperately wished that magic did work on inanimate objects. Just as she thought it, the engine started.

'Yay!' everyone cheered. They all jumped in the car and Signor Moscari turned it round to go back up the hill as that was the correct direction for Florence.

Nadia and Elena burbled excitedly all the way. Even Nadia's parents were thrilled by the excursion but Marcy was too tense to join in the fun. They were just half an hour late, but that could cost them their place in the queue.

'Are you sure you feel all right, Marcella?' Signora Moscari asked.

'Yeah, I'm fine.'

'You don't look fine. Would you like us to stop for a bit?'

'I don't think that's a good idea, actually,' Signor Moscari said. 'We might not get the car going again.'

'Well maybe we should take her home?'

'No, no, I don't want to go home. I'm just not used to the excitement, that's all.'

'Well, if you're sure. If you change your mind, just

let us know.'

'Okay, I will,' Marcy said more chirpily. If Nadia's parents got too concerned, they would turn the car around and it would be over. She tried to smile and sing along with Nadia and Elena.

There was a massive queue outside the studio. Marcy's heart sank. So did everyone else's. 'Oh, no!' the Moscaris groaned.

'We've come too far to go back now,' Signora Moscari said. 'We may as well try queuing if everyone's happy to do that.'

'Yes!' the girls all yelled determinedly. They walked to the back of the queue.

'All right, that's it, I'm afraid. No more for "Ecco Enrico!" now,' a security guard shouted as they approached. Marcy's heart banged angrily. To have got so close was just the worst thing!

'Oh, please let us through!' she cried, but the security guard wasn't listening. He completely ignored her and walked past her. He pulled a barrier across the road just behind them. They were the last people allowed in the queue. They had just made it! They had an hour's wait until seven o'clock when they would start letting the audience in. They had brought food which they ate while they waited; a standing-up picnic.

Once the food was gone, it was the longest hour of Marcy's life. The only thing she had to do to fill the time was reach her hand into her pocket to check that she had still got her potion-endowed item. She had brought Luke a change of clothes in a shoulder bag, but she didn't think it would be wise to give him the bag while he was a donkey as it would undoubtedly be taken from him. She put her faith in him wearing a costume again, which he could use in the meantime.

Finally, the queue began to shuffle into the studio. The queue snaked slowly through the impressive foyer. The walls were covered in giant stills and portraits from its most famous show, "Ecco Enrico!". They were mostly shots from the Signor Donkey skits, though it couldn't always have been that way. Marcy wondered how long they would remain after Signor Donkey – fingers crossed – disappeared without a trace.

Up ahead Marcy could see that the queue split into four according to the various seating areas: top left, top right, bottom left and bottom right. It was important to her plan that she was near the front and next to an aisle. Nadia's family didn't object to being near the front so they agreed to ask to be sat where Marcy wanted.

Unfortunately, they had no such luck. Being the last people in, there weren't even five seats together for them. The family was told that they would have to be split up. Marcy made sure that she was first in out of the five of them so that she could pick the best of the remaining seats.

Once the audience was settled, the floor manager made an announcement: 'Now then, first of all, remember that we are here to entertain you and you are here to enjoy yourselves. But we're also *all* here to make sure that the people at home enjoy the show. So here's what we're going to do. We're going to run the opening titles and you're going to watch me and when I raise my hands, you'll all clap. Then you go quiet and there's a roll of drums and the announcer says "And now, the clown you've all been waiting for... ecco… Enrico!". I'll raise my hands and you clap and cheer. After that, it's very simple. You laugh when you're amused and clap before and after every act. Right, let's practise the beginning. And... cue titles.'

The opening music ran. Marcy was probably unique in being the only person to have heard it only once before. The floor manager raised his hands towards the end of the piece and everyone clapped.

'Aw, that was pathetic. I thought you liked this show! Come on, louder! We'll try again. Cue titles.'

History repeated itself, but this time the applause was a bit louder, a bit more confident.

'That's better. You're getting there, but it's still not good enough. Really let your hair down this time. Go mad!'

Marcy wished they would just get on with it.

'Okay, that'll have to do, we're out of time. Right everyone, relax and enjoy the show.'

The floor manager buzzed about for five minutes, checking in with camera operators and other people like him with headsets and clipboards. Marcy peered at the wings eagerly to see if there was any sign of Luke yet. There wasn't.

'Okay, folks,' the floor manager returned. 'We're going to go in one minute, so remember what we practised and can we have quiet now please?'

The audience went from one extreme to the other. They were deathly quiet one minute and cheering ecstatically the next.

Marcy stood out from the crowd. She didn't care to wave to the camera that swept over the audience. She wasn't bothered about cheering for a star she barely knew or the childish acts he performed. She just wanted to see Luke. But time passed and there was no sign of the donkey.

'We're going to take a break now,' Enrico said. 'But join us right after for Signor Donkey.'

The audience whooped and hollered.

'Please stay in your seats!' the floor manager called. 'We're not off air for long.'

Enrico drank some water and had his make-up touched up. Marcy searched again for some sign of

Luke but there was none. At least he would be on soon.

Luke still hadn't appeared by the second set of adverts.
Enrico had realised what a huge draw the donkey was
and was saving him until near the end. It meant that the
audience at home had to watch all of the show to avoid
missing Signor Donkey and it would prevent people
switching off as soon as they had seen the donkey. It
was better for advertising revenue that way. It also
meant that Enrico could build up the tension so that
Signor Donkey would be even funnier.

The tension was certainly building up for Marcy. She
was stressed enough without having to wait until the
end of the show to carry out her plan. But, with no
other sign of Luke, she had no choice but to anxiously
wait until after his official appearance.

'And now it's time for... Signor Donkey!'

At last! The audience screamed. Marcy sat upright
in her seat. The video screens in the studio went black
and then portrayed the caption: "Too many donkeys
spoil the broth". Signor Donkey was dressed in a
dinner suit with an apron over the top.

'Hello,' said Renata Galbrigio, the famous and
beautiful TV chef. She too was dressed in glamorous
evening wear beneath a "Tastes of the World" apron.
'Today on "Tastes of the World" I'm joined by Signor
Donkey,' she continued.

'Ee-orr.'

'Nice to meet you too. Now then, Signor Donkey,
you're keen on all sorts of foods from around the world,
aren't you?'

The donkey nodded his head.

'And I hear you're a bit of an expert in the kitchen
too.'

The donkey nodded his head and brayed.

'Good. Now then, I thought today we'd cook something from closer to home. How about spaghetti Bolognese?'

'Ee-orr.'

'Right. Well, as you can see, the pasta's already boiling away in that pan there. And in this pan I've made up the delicious, authentic sauce. You can get the recipe details from my website or on the "Tastes of the World" app. Signor Donkey, could you just stir that for me while I get the plates out?'

'Ee-orr.' He picked up the wooden spoon between his teeth and stirred the sauce, dilating his nostrils and absorbing the aroma with an appreciative nod of his head. The audience laughed.

'Right, time to serve up!' Renata held the pasta pot while the donkey picked up a spaghetti spoon and somehow managed to extricate some spaghetti and dump it on the plates before too much of it fell off. Then he served up some of the sauce and meatballs. Renata carried the plates over to a romantically set table and the audience 'whoo'ed. Renata stripped their aprons off and tied a napkin around Luke's neck. The donkey, ever the perfect gentleman, used his teeth to pull her chair out for her, then parked his hind quarters on the floor in his usual manner.

'You know, this is a dream come true for me, Signor Donkey,' Renata said.

'Ee-orr?'

'Just you and me, some fine food and wine. A little romantic music...' she snapped her fingers and violinists approached and played their instruments. She picked up a large wineglass and handed it to Signor Donkey. He took it between his teeth. Then she picked her own glass up and said 'Here's to us'. They toasted themselves and the donkey tipped his head back and guzzled down the wine. He swayed comically at its effect.

Signor Donkey proceeded to eat his spaghetti as he had done at Enrico's house, licking his lips clean to the rapturous delight of the audience. Renata got up and lovingly wiped his face clean with his napkin.

'And now, a little kiss, darling,' she said sultrily, throwing her arms around his neck. The donkey puckered up his mouth and gave her a big smack on the lips, winking at the camera. The shot was frozen and "The End" was captioned over it on the video screens. The end was greeted with the usual mad clamour and Enrico desperately shouting: 'Thanks for watching. Catch us on Thursday when we'll be back with Signor Donkey!'

'Oh no you won't,' Marcy muttered under the closing theme of the show. It was time to put her plan into action.

11 LUKE GOES BALD

Marcy stood up hastily and charged down the centre aisle. The audience didn't notice what she was doing as they were too engrossed in their applause. Fortunately some people even stood up to show their appreciation, masking Marcy's movements from the security guards. It was going well so far. She reached into her pocket as she ran and grasped what was inside. She pulled it carefully from her pocket, struggling slightly as the awkwardly long object lodged itself in the material. She gripped it as hard as she dared once she had extricated it, afraid she would drop it now that the crucial moment was at hand.

Having made it onto the stage floor, people finally began to notice Marcy. The audience's applause was gradually replaced by the murmur of shocked gasps. The security guards lurched into action but Marcy was way ahead of them. She shouted 'Luke!' and the donkey halted his progress off stage and turned his head inquisitively round. He recognised Marcy instantly and his eyes widened in surprise. His lifted his nose into the air and let out an excited bray.

Marcy proffered the carrot made of orange icing sugar, urgently whispering: 'Keep this in your mouth and eat it *as soon* as you're alone and you'll change back straight away. Use the clothes you've got on for now. We'll be waiting by the back stage door. Okay?'

Luke nodded his head.

'Good. I'll see you later then.'

Two security guards looped their arms under hers and walked her off backwards.

'I just wanted to give him a carrot!' Marcy protested to them. 'He's so wonderful! I just love him!'

'Well I'm afraid you're not allowed to do that sort of thing, young lady.'

'Am I in a lot of trouble?' Marcy asked, a quaver in her voice.

'Not a lot. Just banned from coming back to the studio.'

Marcy gulped. She checked her watch. In just over two hours the magic carrot would lose its potency. She hoped that Luke had understood the urgency of eating it quickly. What would she do if this plan failed? Now that she was banned from the studio, it had to work!

'Marcella! Are you all right? What did you go and do that for?' Signora Moscari shrilled when they were finally reunited in the foyer.

'I'm fine. I just wanted to meet Signor Donkey and give him a carrot. I didn't think there would be anything wrong with it. They'd finished filming and everything.'

'Well, you nearly gave us a heart attack. Phew. I had no idea you were such a big fan. After all, it's only the second time you've seen the show.'

'I know, but it's great, isn't it? And Enrico's so wonderful! I'd love to get his autograph.'

'Ooh, yeah, that'd be cool. Everyone at school

would be sooo jealous. Do you think Enrico'll leave by the back door? We could wait there and grab him when he comes out,' Nadia suggested, much to Marcy's pleasure.

'Hey, yeah. It'd be great if we could!' she said exuberantly.

'Can we Mum?' Nadia asked.

'No, I don't think so.' Marcy's face fell. 'We've done enough waiting around today and we've seen what we came to see. It'll already be late by the time we get home so we'd better get going now.'

'Yeah, but since we've come so far we might as well take the opportunity while we're here. It'd really make the trip one to remember. And it'd really cheer Marcella up. She's been really upset since Luke went missing.'

'Yes, and so has her dad and if I don't get Marcella home on time, he'll worry that she's gone missing too.'

'Aww, no one really expects you to get home exactly when you said you would. Please can we wait just half an hour? Pleeeease?'

'Oh, go on then. Half an hour, no more.'

'Thanks Mum, you're brilliant!'

'Yes, thanks!' Marcy enthused. Perfect! She just hoped that half an hour would buy enough time for Luke.

Luke was led off stage and back to his celebrity dressing room. He hoped he would be left alone as soon as possible as it wasn't very comfortable keeping the carrot in his mouth and the sweetness of it was making him drool. He could feel his skin tingling with the potion as he sucked on it.

'Right then, love,' his assistant said. 'Let's get these things off you.'

Luke shook his head adamantly.

'No? You don't want them off?'

Luke shook his head again and put his ears back flat.

'Well, love, you're going to have to, I'm afraid. Costume won't be happy if you get this covered in straw and dung.' She made a move to unbutton the dinner jacket and Luke swung his head round at her, baring his teeth in warning.

'Don't you get narky with me!' the assistant said, slapping him smartly on the nose. Luke lifted his hind leg and made a restrained kick with it to show his displeasure.

'Oi! Give up!'

Luke wished the assistant would give up. This was taking too long. He ran circles around her, trying to keep as much distance between her and his clothes as possible. She made grabs at his mane in order to catch him, but when she succeeded all she had to show for it was a handful of detached hair. She stared at it in alarm and then realised that there were fairy clumps of hair floating round the room that had been dislodged by the chase.

'Uh-oh, I don't think you're very well are you? No wonder you're behaving funny. I'd better go and fetch the vet!' She bustled out of the room.

Luke used his long tongue to manoeuvre the melted mush of icing sugar that was now firmly stuck to the roof of his mouth. It was a difficult task which wasn't made any easier by the rush he was in. He caught sight of his gurning face in the mirror and paused in his tongue twisting to look at the rest of his reflection. He really was a sight, with bald patches all over his visible coat.

He felt a strange chill as he shed the rest of his hair inside his costume. All that was left was a patch of mane on the top of his head. As he swallowed the last of the potion he could feel his body become elastic and bendy. And this time he could watch it mutate too. His ears and tail shrank back into his body. His front hoofs shrank slightly and thumbs grew out of the heels. He used those thumbs to hold his costume up around him. His fingers re-formed and joined in his efforts to maintain his modesty.

His concave back arched and shortened. His joints reversed so that the elbows on his hind legs became knees and the knees on his forelegs became elbows. The most sickening half-change of all was that Luke's human face returned, but his head maintained a donkey shape. Luke shuddered and felt his still-thick skin tingle with goosebumps.

Luke realised that he didn't have time to waste staring at his disgusting hybrid form. The assistant could be back with the vet at any moment. Now that he had two legs again, it was time to high-tail it – unsteadily – through the doorway.

After an anxious quarter of an hour's wait by the back door, it opened and a gangly adolescent clutching a mass of black cloth tripped through it. He rolled onto his back and looked up at the people surrounding him.

'It's Luke!' Marcy said, pretending as though she was taken utterly by surprise.

'Is it?!' Signora Moscari asked, peering closer.

'Hi,' Luke said, grinning sheepishly and he got to his feet, gathering the excessive folds of black material around him. He hadn't expected a welcoming party, just Marcy. Marcy launched herself at him and gave him a giant hug. Thank God it had worked!

'What are you doing here? And what are you wearing?' Signor Moscari asked.

'Err… the guys stole my clothes again. I just grabbed whatever I could, I was in a hurry to try and catch you guys before you left. I was hoping you could take me back to Caravalla.'

'But where have you been all this time?'

'I'll tell you on the way back,' Luke said to encourage them to move. He didn't want to be hanging around in Signor Donkey's costume when they found the animal was missing.

'We're waiting for Enrico,' Nadia told him.

'Oh, come on,' Marcy said, taking Luke's arm and leading him away. 'They'll come after us.' She realised the clothes she had brought Luke were useless since everyone would now question why she had brought them and she had no idea how to explain where Luke had been. She sincerely hoped that Luke didn't intend telling them the truth.

Marcy led Luke off in the direction of the car park. Nadia's family stood about giving each other confused looks. They were especially puzzled by the trails of brown fur Luke was depositing from under his fabric. With no answers to be found where they were, the Moscaris started to follow the pair.

'Are you all right?' Marcy asked Luke as they walked.

'Not really. This loose hair's making me all itchy.'

'And there I was thinking you'd be grateful to be human again. I suppose you were enjoying the fame?'

'Nah. Fame's only worth it if you get paid for it, and all I got was a few square meals and a snog! And I am grateful. Thanks. Really, thank you. It's just all happened so suddenly.'

'You're not going to tell them what really happened are you?' Marcy asked Luke.

'I suppose not. But what can I say?'

'I dunno. At first everyone thought that the thieves had kidnapped you but they swore blind they hadn't, of course. Then people thought that maybe you'd tried to get back to England because you were homesick. But when you didn't turn up there they began to fear the worst. They thought that maybe the bandits had killed you, which was why they were denying ever having anything to do with you. But your friends thought Mum had turned you into a frog! Crazy, huh?'

'As if,' Luke joked back.

'I suppose you can tell everyone that the thieves did kidnap you but you –'

Marcy was interrupted by the arrival of the Moscaris, so it was all down to Luke now. She hoped that whatever story he came up with would be convincing.

If there had been arguments before about who was sitting where in the car, it was even more awkward now that there were six of them to squeeze in.

'You'll just have to sit on Nadia's knee, Elena,' Signor Moscari said.

'I don't see why *I* should have to sit on someone's knee,' Elena said. 'Luke's the one who's not supposed to be here. *He* can sit on someone's knee.'

'Elena! Stop being so bad mannered to a guest,' Signora Moscari scolded.

'And silly, ' Nadia added. 'Luke's too big for that.'

'Someone can come and get him later,' Elena retorted. 'He chose to run away, I don't see why we should have to put up with him.'

'Elena!' Signora Moscari scolded again. 'Stop being so insensitive. We don't know what Luke's been through. And we're certainly not leaving him behind.'

'Yeah! Shut up, or we'll leave *you* behind and see how you like it,' Nadia jibed.

'Nadia!' said Signora Moscari.

'Huh!' said Elena, sitting with all her force on her sister's knee and crossly folding her arms once Nadia had got the seatbelt around them both.

Signor Moscari started the now obedient engine and set off as soon as Luke and Marcy were strapped in.

'So, Luke, what did happen?' he asked. 'Where've

you been for the past couple of months? It must be some story.'

'Not really. But I'd rather tell it when we get back to Caravalla to save me having to go through it twice,' Luke answered.

Marcy thought that was a clever way of playing for time.

Everyone was quiet on the way home. Elena was sulking and Nadia had no-one to talk to as both Luke and Marcy were too busy trying to think of the best way to sort things out.

They knew their adventure wasn't over yet...

12 MORE CONCOCTIONS

When the Moscaris' car arrived at Riccardo's house they all saw a police car outside. Luke and Marcy's hearts jumped. Were the police there to arrest them in connection with the disappearance of the celebrity donkey?

As soon as they heard the car outside the gates, Serena, Riccardo and Sergeant Morabelle came bounding out of the house. Marcy was first out of the car, having been squashed against the door, and she was swept up in Riccardo's arms.

'Oh, Marcella! You're all right! I was worried something had happened to you. That would have been typical, having my only child taken from me on top of all that's happened!'

'Dad! I'm only an hour late! You're so silly. Why is Sergeant Morabelle here?'

'When you didn't come home I rode into town to tell them you'd gone missing.'

'I can't believe you did that!'

'I told him not to, but you know what he's like. When he gets an idea in his head...' Serena shrugged her shoulders and rolled her eyes back.

'I knew I shouldn't have agreed to let you go.'

'Dad, stop it. Anyway, it was all worth it. Look who I found!'

On cue, being well trained in performing now, Luke stepped out of the car. He was greeted with overwhelming enthusiasm, a cacophony of 'Are you alright?'s and 'Thank God's.

'Well it's a good job I'm here after all,' Sergeant Morabelle said. 'We'll need to take a statement from you, Luke, about where you've been, and then that should be the case closed. At last!'

Sergeant Morabelle was glad he wouldn't have to deal with the frantic Riccardo anymore. At least his wife was always calm. Unnervingly so, sometimes. Still, she must be a good influence on Riccardo, though it was surprising that she could put up with him. She seemed too good for the life she led, but perhaps that was what enabled her to rise above Riccardo's trivial catastrophes.

Everyone went inside, including the Moscaris. Coffee was made while Luke put some proper clothes on. He gratefully disposed of the incriminating costume in the autumn fire burning in Marcy's bedroom grate. Despite the late hour, everyone sat around their storytelling hero, eager-eared.

'Well, I was kidnapped by the thieves when they burgled Riccardo's house to be used as insurance against getting caught while they made their getaway.'

'But the thieves deny ever having laid eyes on you!' Sergeant Morabelle interjected.

'Probably because they thought they could get away with lying after what they did to me. I struggled against being kidnapped so they hit me on the head. When I woke up I was in a really run-down wooden house.' Luke's description of the house proved to the Sergeant that Luke had indeed been there. 'I couldn't remember anything, not even my name, but I guessed I was a prisoner because I was tied up. But the thieves all fell asleep after they had had their dinner and I managed to free myself and escape.

'Of course, I didn't know where to escape to, since I had lost my memory, so I just hitched lifts to Florence. I had to sleep on the streets for a few nights as I didn't have any money and no one would help me.'

'Why didn't you go to the police?' everyone except Marcy chimed in at once.

'Er…well…' Luke squirmed at this unexpected, yet obvious ginormous hole in his story. 'I've no idea!' he answered honestly.

'I suppose you weren't thinking too straight after the bump on the head,' Riccardo suggested for him, much to Luke's relief. 'I know I didn't feel right for days after those nasty men bashed *me* on the head.'

'But didn't you see the missing person posters, Luke? We put them all over the place, Florence included.' Sergeant Morabelle said.

'Well, I got in with a group of homeless guys who sleep in the film studios in winter. We got in by queuing up to be in the audience of a TV show, but then we sneaked into the storage area where we could sleep without being seen. We didn't go outside again. During the day we could rummage through all the cool stuff they kept in there, and there was plenty of leftover food lying around and toilets and showers and everything.

'Whilst I was washing today the guys nicked my clothes as a joke - they did that a lot, picking on me 'cause I was the newest. I couldn't run around with no clothes on so they eventually agreed to nick me something from the costume department, and thought it would be funny to get me a big black dress. They wouldn't give me my clothes back unless I went to watch "Ecco Enrico" being recorded in the dress.

'So I sat in the audience and after the show I saw a girl run down to give the donkey a carrot and I thought she looked familiar and then everything suddenly came back to me.

'I tried to get to Marcy but she was carted off by the security guards. I couldn't follow since I wasn't properly dressed so I ran out of the back door in the hope that I would still find her, and there she was! With the Moscaris. It was great, like they'd all been waiting for me!'

'We were waiting for Enrico,' Elena said crossly. 'And we didn't get to meet him because of you. It's not fair!'

'I'm sorry about that, Elena. But I'm very glad to know who I am again and be back here. And now I can go home.'

'Yes, yes. Your grandparents came here after you disappeared, but you were gone so long they had to go home. But we'll notify them straight away. The constables at the station should be able to phone them and relay our radio signal so you can talk to your family just now, let them know you're safe. They'll be so relieved. And we'll get your head looked at at the hospital to check there's no permanent damage. And organise a flight home as soon as possible,' Sergeant Morabelle said. 'But you'll have to come back to Italy to testify in court when the case against your kidnappers comes up.'

Luke nodded his head. He'd worry about that another day. Right now, he would talk to his family, and then he just wanted a good night's sleep.

Although he had been treated like royalty lately, it was still a luxury to lie in a proper bed in his proper shape. And as much as he had missed it, it was strange being human again. He had got used to being a donkey. He felt deaf now as human hearing was so bad. He wanted to rotate his ears in order to hear people better. And he was suffering from all the other donkey impulses: he wanted to twitch his skin when he had an itch and scratch behind his ear with his leg. He hoped he'd feel more human in the morning.

'You're not going to sleep are you?' Marcy asked Luke incredulously when he blew out the lamp.

'Er - yes! I'm shattered.'

'But I'm dying to hear your real story!'

'It'll have to wait 'til the morning.'

'There might not be time in the morning. You heard. Hospitals and flights back to England tomorrow. And the sooner you leave the better in case the police check your story out and find it's not true.'

'Then I'll just write to you when I get home.'

'I can't wait that long! And we need to figure out how to stop my mum doing magic. It was your fault you got into that mess, you know, guzzling that potion down like a… well, like an ass! I've helped you and now you owe me one.'

'Yes, I know. And believe me, I've had plenty of time to think about my crime! But wait 'til morning! *Please,*' Luke groaned.

'Well, just make sure you're up early enough.'

She was answered by a snore.

Marcy shook Luke awake.

'Ehuhhh…' he groaned, distinctly donkey-like. With his increasing awareness he managed to articulate: 'What time is it?'.

'It's morning. Come on, get up. You said you would.'

Luke rolled over and picked up his old watch. 'Morning?! Four o'clock in the morning! I've only been in bed for two and a half hours. You can wake me at nine.' He thrust his head under his sheets.

'No!' Marcy wailed. 'Mum's up on the roof now! She woke me up when she climbed the stairs. Come on! Let's go up there and confront her.' She began shaking Luke again.

'Oh, for goodness sake! All right then.' Luke crawled out of bed and rubbed his eyes sleepily. Then the pyjama-clad pair crept quietly up to their position behind the rainwater tank.

Serena was busy making up another owl concoction.

'Go and ask her what she's doing,' Luke instructed Marcy.

'No.'

'Yes! Come on, I'll back you up.'

'But I don't know what to say.'

'Oh, stop dithering. Let's get it over with so I can get back to bed. Come on.'

They stepped out from their hiding place. Serena caught their movement instantly. 'You two! What are you doing up here? Get back to bed!'

'What are you up to, Mum?'

'Nothing to do with you.'

'But I'm worried. I don't want you to transform more sheep or anything. I don't think it's right.'

'And I heard the thieves say they found a secret stash of money under your bed,' Luke chipped in.

'Dad knew nothing about that when Sergeant Morabelle mentioned it, so you must have had something to do with it,' Marcy continued.

'I don't have to explain myself to you. I'm your mother, and you'll do as I tell you. Now forget about all of this and go back to bed.' Serena glared at them.

Luke looked at Marcy who appeared ready to obey. He nudged her in the back and whispered 'Oh, be brave little Miss Goody-goody. It's the only way to get this sorted.'

'I'm not going back to bed until we sort this out,' Marcy boldly told Serena. 'And if you don't tell me, I'll tell Dad.'

'Dad would probably thank me! If it wasn't for me, this farm would have gone the same way the others are going around here, only a lot faster.'

'What do you mean? Aren't you the one causing the blight on everyone's vineyards?' Luke demanded.

'Of course not. I've told you before I don't want to make anyone suffer. I just don't want *us* to suffer. We worked so, so hard for years yet we were as poor as we'd always been. We've got the worst land around here so nothing we did made much of a difference. And then there's my sister in Florence with her big house and lots of money and she can give Marcella's cousins anything they want. I hate not being able to give you anything, Marcella. And I'm tired of living such a hard life.'

'I know our life isn't easy, Mum, but I like it that we earn a living from making things grow and caring for them,' Marcy said softly.

'When your Gran died and I inherited her spell book I didn't see any harm in casting a spell to protect our crops from the blight. I haven't cursed anyone else's. And I've made some small changes to help make us more efficient, like with Arturo's sheep. We've made sacrifices too like going without electricity, and even food sometimes. I scrimped and saved all our money and managed to keep it hidden from Dad 'cause he's not very good with money. Then it was all taken from me by a bunch of crooks. And with Luke's disappearance and all the attention on our house I haven't been able to do anything. So now Luke's back safely I'm just going to fly to Borenze Police Station and get back what's rightfully ours.'

'It's not rightfully ours!' Marcy burst out. 'It's money

you've made by witchcraft and by stealing things from other people.'

'They're just little things, Marcella, of no importance to anyone else. But it will mean we can afford to move to a nice house in a decent town and you can have a proper childhood.'

'But I like living in the country and I like my friends here. And what about Dad? His life revolves around being hard done by. He wouldn't be the same if you took that away from him. You never asked either of us if we wanted to be rich.'

'So you're telling me you don't want to have electricity or a television? You don't want some new clothes?'

'Of course I want them. But I want to get them a more honest way.'

'As I said, we tried everything we could. I've had it up to here with your Aunt Anna nagging me for marrying for love instead of for money. I hate it when we go to see her in our tatty clothes and she shows off all their new things to us. I'm fed up of being too ashamed of this rickety old place to invite her here. And you've got no idea how hurtful it is when she accuses me of depriving you. I feel like a terrible mother!'

'No you're not! You're always calm and sensible and you're always there for me when I have a problem. There must be a way of making all of us happy. If Dad's not good with money, you should keep looking after it. We'll soon save up enough to do up the house. Then you can have Aunt Anna over and we'll show them how happy we are with what we've got. That's all I want - for us all to be happy.'

'Are you sure?'

'Definitely. And I'm sure that Dad wants the same. He likes to complain, but really he's proud of being honest and humble.'

'Yes, you are right about that. It's one of the things I've always loved about him.'

'Good. So you can forget about becoming an owl.'

Serena shifted uncomfortably, reluctant to relinquish her hard-saved cash. 'How about we use that money to get power installed and a television?'

'Only if you promise not to use witchcraft anymore.' Marcy bargained, secretly glad to be able to afford such luxuries.

'But what about the farm? Our vineyard will fail like everyone else's next year if I don't use magic to protect them.'

'Then why not use magic to protect everyone's vines?' Marcy suggested.

'But it'll take me ages to make that much health-giving potion!' Serena protested. 'And to fly over everyone's fields to water their crops with it. I've got enough to do as it is.'

'I'll help,' Marcy offered. 'Agreed?'

'Agreed.'

Marcy went to Serena and they hugged and kissed.

'Also,' Marcy said, 'do you think you could turn Luke into an owl for a bit? We spied on you last time you did it and he was so desperate to try it that he drank the wrong potion and turned into a donkey!' Marcy thought she might as well get the confession out of the way while her mum was filled with maternal love.

'So that's where he's been all this time!' Serena laughed. 'Marcella, why didn't you tell me?'

'I was going to! But since you couldn't help I didn't see what the point was, other than getting myself into trouble.'

'That must have been a heavy secret to keep to yourself. What happened to me being someone you can always turn to? Next time, don't hesitate to come to me, will you? Even if there's nothing I can do, you know the saying: "A problem shared is a problem halved"?'

'You're right,' Marcy conceded happily. She knew now why her mum was the way she was, and most importantly that she really did care about them all. That was a good start to their happy ever after.

'Well thank goodness you're okay, Luke,' Serena said. 'Are you going to tell us what really happened while you were gone? Luke?'

They turned to look at Luke. He was balanced on one leg, resting the other, and snoring quietly away.

ABOUT THE AUTHOR

Photo by John Hollingsworth

Alison has enjoyed creative writing in all forms since she was a child, and has had poems and a short story published, a play produced, and was short-listed in several writing competitions.

Alison studied English, Scottish and Classical literature at the University of St Andrews. Whilst there, she read an old translation of Apuleius's *The Golden Ass* (for fun), and saw its potential to be re-written as a children's story. She wrote the first draft of what is now called *The Exchange Trip* in 2001. The book had mostly sat dormant ever since, until the Covid-19 lockdown of spring 2020 provided plenty of free time for Alison to dust it off, finally come up with a suitable title, and publish it.

This is Alison's first children's book and she is currently working on another adventure for Luke Silvester.

Alison is also writing a series of stories about family pets for younger readers, starting with *Coco the Cat*.

Alison aims to support charity by donating the royalties from *The Exchange Trip* and *Coco the Cat*, and providing copies to not-for-profits to sell or auction to raise their own funds. Please visit dipitus.wordpress.com to find out more.

Printed in Poland
by Amazon Fulfillment
Poland Sp. z o.o., Wrocław

64191062R00080